La Rose
Le Baton Chronicles

Claudia Helena Ross

Blame Helena Books and Media
San Diego, California

www.blamehelenabooks.com

To my Little Girl Jordan who sat on Auntie's lap as she wrote this book

Prologue

Out of habit, he removed his watch from his vest. The timepiece possessed no hands. He sighed, returning it to his pocket. Barachiel understood time ceased to exist in the Garden, but he couldn't help to check anyway. He hated being kept waiting, but he had no choice. Pacing a bit, he returned to the fountain once more. He knew what he would find there, but he couldn't resist the temptation of looking inside anyway. Empty and dry, as expected.

"Mon Frère?"

"Oui?"

Raguel arched his brow, admonishing Barachiel for his earthly attire with his eyes. "We are in the presence of the Most High. Have you forgotten, *mon Frère?*"

"Oh. Oui, mon Frère." Barachiel's clothing melted away, returning him to his natural angelic form. Concerned about his appearance, he ran to the garden's lake to check his reflection. He admired his white tunic, emblazoned with a silk embroidered red rose, soaring up high from his lower ab-domen to his neckline, crossed by a golden sword to its left and a budding baton to its right, all centered within a golden crown. Barachiel adjusted his belt, comprised of fine gold-en threads braided together forming a rope, completed with ruby adorned tassels. Standing up straight, he adjusted his belt so it wouldn't disturb the embroidered emblem upon his chest.

He considered his feathers. His wings, nearly touching the lawn, seemed perfect. He had yet to detect a gray feath-er. Satisfied with his immaculate attire, Barachiel returned to the fountain.

"You're vain."

"I'm not, Raguel. We can't all be as humble as you," he said. "But then again, I suppose we all are, for we are all ser-vants of the Most High."

Raguel wandered away, coming to rest upon a marble bench. *He'll wrinkle his tunic,* Barachiel fretted, but then he realized Raguel wouldn't. How could a wrinkle exist within the Lord's Garden? He admired Raguel's tunic, the Ark of the Covenant stitched in gold upon it, in all its glory, back dropped with a small pastoral scene of the Ethiopian lands. He loved how the gold embroidery seemed to highlight Raguel's brown complexion, giving his appearance a radiant glow.

His feathers were the most beautiful hue of brown Barachiel had ever beheld, the color of rich, sweet chocolate. The brown barbs interlaced with the gold barbules gave his wings an almost iridescent glow. Barachiel laughed a bit to himself, understanding. Yes, that was it; Barachiel determined. Raguel's complexion had absorbed the golden hue of the Ark.

An emerald green light blinded Barachiel and Raguel, but they recovered. Barachiel took heart, finding his brother before him. *"Bienvenue, mon Frère,"* Barachiel said with a shout. It had been some time since he'd seen his brother.

"Greetings, mon Frère."

Barachiel was pleased to find Sealtiel attired in his Throne Room best. He admired his long mustache, completely white, as was his hair which coursed down to his feet, trailing the lawn behind him as he approached Barachiel. Sealtiel's tunic displayed a jade altar, embellished with fierce dragons, their snouts aimed up towards heaven, meeting at a point, supporting an open tomb topped by a crown with a fish suspended above it. The pastoral lands of China were displayed in the background. A woman in traditional Chinese garb stood before the altar holding a rose in her hand, presenting it to heaven. "It is good to see you this day, mon Frère," Barachiel greeted him.

"Good to see you, as well."

A cold wind coursed through the Garden, causing the edges of the flowers' leaves and petals to brown and wither. A handsome man appeared before the group. Hatred, arrogance, and greed emanated from him, although he made an attempt to mask the evil vibration. "Bienvenue, mon Frère." Barachiel walked over to his brother and patted him on the back. "I didn't believe you'd be able to re-arrange your calendar. I'm glad to see you could accommodate us today."

Mammon scowled at him, turning away. He refused to give Barachiel the satisfaction of a reply. Barachiel always found his imprisonments entertaining. In any case, his day of exaltation rapidly approached. Barachiel would prove incapable of sarcasm on that day.

"Would you care to change?" Barachiel asked him.

Mammon mutated into his natural form, the mark of his master rising upon his forehead.

Barachiel detested his garb, a bland colored tunic detailed with a green swirl of some sort. A clinched fist burst forth from the center of the swirl grasping at coins, with some falling away. His skin appeared as boiled flesh. His wings were bare without feathers, sporting the same boiled skin, its skeleton protruding through. His wings were pitifully small. Perhaps the size of his wings indicated the size of his 'manhood.'

"I assure you I'm generously endowed," Mammon said,

in reply to Barachiel's thoughts.

"Not as I am," Barachiel said. He stretched his wings and walked away.

Although he loved his existence as an archangel, Barachiel had enjoyed his days walking the earth in the male form. Well, most of them, anyway. Many of his brothers had chosen to operate as males while assisting the Lord's little ones, archangels and fallen angels alike.

Only the Sisters had chosen the female form, but it seemed to work for them. Then again, they only interacted with *L'Order de la Rose*, the Children of Israel's anointed, the Christ and the Most High. Their work didn't require them to labor amongst the masses, as with the rest of them. In these elite circles, no man would discriminate against the Sisters due to their chosen sex.

Archangels and fallen angels alike desired to blend in with the children of God. Humans rarely embraced anyone different in appearance from themselves, let alone heeding any advice or guidance offered by such a person. In most instances, society perceived these outsiders as invaders or as a threat to their safety and their way of life. As a result, the angels working in locales north of the Equator typically adopted physiques with a paler skin color while those working with men of the southern hemisphere adorned browner hues.

Spotting a shadow on the lawn, Barachiel turned his eyes towards heaven. A dove glided down. Circling a bit, the bird came to rest upon the rim of the stone fountain. When the four brothers approached his perch, the bird flew away.

Water flowed into the fount, the Word of God unfolding into the natural world. The Spirit churned the water, forcing a vapor to rise, filling the Garden with its mist. They swooned.

The four revived once the mist lifted, finding the water frozen within the fountain. "Release the Word of the Most High," Raguel said. The water returned to its liquid state. Now still and placid, it became a window to the future.

The four peered within, observing. Mammon snickered. "I hold him."

"You can't see as we can, mon Frère. You've already lost, as the Most High declared at the Beginning," Barachiel said.

"Allow us to begin; I will prove my words are true," Mammon said.

Raguel gritted his teeth. How could an archangel be such a fool? "Believe in your lie if you so desire. You can't take Le Baton; however, the Most High will allow you the opportunity to prove to yourself that his Word is so." Raguel suppressed his almost irresistible desire to slay him. "In any case, the Most High's Rose will not allow you to take her child. She may just slay you before the end." Raguel began to laugh, soon joined by Barachiel and Sealtiel.

"Yes, and the Keyholder isn't the fool you believe him to be," Barachiel said. "Much like you, he possesses neither a heart nor a conscience. However, will this aversive personality trait in the child work to your benefit?"

The men continued to gaze into the fount. Barachiel, Sealtiel, and Raguel rejoiced and grieved for the future of their little ones.

Mammon scowled, containing his rage. "The Rose's Keyholder will surrender his Seed to me. In the end, he will give me his Key."

As Barachiel continued to peer into the fount, he sensed Raguel's uneasiness. "Do not fret, Raguel. Remember, God always protects his Seed."

Mammon scoffed at Barachiel's testimony. "Let us begin," he said.

"Yes. We shall begin," Barachiel said. They all dipped their fingers into the warm water together, gliding their hands through. The water swirled, draining from the fountain.

With the future envisioned and their respective missions defined, they each departed the Garden in opposite directions, destined for a common end.

PART I

Chapter 1

New Orleans, Louisiana. August 27, 1963

"I would rather go to Hell, than to have returned here, to New Orleans." The bartender shot him a dirty look, but he didn't care. He appraised his surroundings in disgust and disbelief. He really didn't understand how he had been roped into returning. Well yeah, he did.

Sipping his Glenlivet, he frowned. "A Carousel? Amazing. It's a bar. Why turn it into a child's amusement park ride?" However, the Hotel Monteleone was famous for it. Apparently, others believed differently than he.

Who would patronize a bar to indulge in the warm and fuzzy comforts of childhood dreams? He considered the matter further. Perhaps it was so. The patrons, including him, had come there to escape the horrors of their realities. In any case, he desired to do so. "At least the bartender pours good drinks." Under normal conditions he would have been a little buzzed. However, the agony of the day which loomed before Julian Charles Chamberie squelched it.

He hadn't thought of New Orleans since leaving the city as a teenager. Well, at least he had convinced himself of such. Back then, he loved going to City Park, visiting the French Quarter for ice cream. Julian laughed, realizing he didn't always despise the town. In fact, as a child, he loved the city. He swirled his scotch in its glass, thinking. He couldn't have been any older than fourteen when his mamère—

"Sir, your car has arrived."

"Thanks," he said to the bellman, finishing his scotch. Although his fifth one, the edge remained. It was going to be a fucked up day and he knew it. He couldn't get around it. "Here's something for your trouble." Julian placed a fifty dollar bill on the bar as he turned to leave.

"Sir, your tab is only—"

"We're square," he said, continuing on his way.

"Yes, sir! Thank you, sir," the bartender said, placing the tip in his pocket.

Julian exited the hotel and waited for his car. Within moments, he noticed a limousine in the standing zone, slinking forward several feet to the entrance of the hotel.

Descending the steps, Julian waited at the curb for the car to stop. As he watched the driver exit the vehicle, Julian felt his vision shift without warning, losing his ability to focus on the objects around him. From a hypnotic realm, Julian watched through a fish eye lens the driver round the front of the vehicle. The persistent French Quarter musk accosted his sinuses and intoxicated him like the scent of his girlfriend, Jannette. Centuries of mildew, coupled with the wood and bricks resisting decay, mingled with the flavor of the muggy salt air, formed a seductive bouquet in his olfactory glands.

His lungs compelled him to inhale and exhale several times in rapid succession, greedy for the air. The aroma transported him to a distant and forgotten place in his memory, which he'd been unaware of until that very moment. Without warning, the seductress released him, allowing him to crash back into the dimension of Earth.

Awaking from the dream, groggy and light-headed, Julian batted his eyes in his effort to reacquaint with the present. Once his vision cleared, he found the driver standing before him with the car door open, waiting for him to enter. It was as if he was a Beefeater before the Queen's castle in England, smartly attired, even for a driver. Julian wondered if he tried to punch the driver, would he flinch.

You may try if you care to, young man

Julian had thought he heard the short, dapper man speak to him, but he remained at attention, waiting for him to enter the car. *Freak.* He entered and reclined into the merciful comfort of the air-conditioned limousine. Its plush, black leather seats soothed him as the car slipped into the late morning traffic on Royal Street.

A few days before, he'd received a telegram from Suzette, Grandmère's longtime maid and companion, stating that his grandmère wished to order her affairs prior to her death. Why now? God! Grandmère retained an army of attorneys and accountants. Why not allow them to do it? It angered him he'd been forced to miss the greatest event in Afro-American history since the Emancipation Proclamation because he had to attend to his grandmère.

Gazing out the limousine window, he recognized many of the landmarks. It surprised him that he remembered the way home. "I thought I'd blocked out all of this years ago."

Home, although beautiful on the outside, brimmed with pain and heartache on the inside. He blinked hard and shook his head, blocking out the memories.

"I'm not going to think about all of that. I'll attend the closing for the house on Thursday. I'll finalize the contracts with the nursing facility. That's it. Oh yeah, I must sign the contracts with Christies and set the auction date." However, things rarely occurred as they should.

Fourth Street. He saw the sign and felt as if someone had hit him in the stomach. "Driver, how much longer until we arrive?"

"Just a few more blocks, sir. Five at the most."

"Thank you." So, his gut was right.

Fast ride

"Sir—"

How did it sneak up on him like this? Somehow, it had slipped up on him. Its presence suffocated him.

"—we're here." The end of the driver's sentence registered in his brain as the man exited the vehicle. The driver opened his door and the humidity engulfed Julian's face like a wet feather pillow. He couldn't breathe for a few seconds, and then his lungs adjusted. Julian stepped out of the limousine.

Although smaller than he remembered, the home still appeared quite imposing to him. One couldn't get any more antebellum than this place. He sighed. *Oh Mamère.*

"Look at you! My, you'se a grown man now! What happened to my li'l boy?"

Julian stared at the middle-aged woman racing down the stairs of the porch to greet him, unsure of her identity. "Baby, it's me. Sissy!"

God, this place has not changed one bit since I left, he complained to himself.

"Charlie Boy?"

"Yes, Sissy?" Remembering his manners, he gave her a

quick hug and a peck on the cheek.

She just kind of looked at him, picking up on his detached energy. However, she put it all aside. "Well, let's get inside outta this heat," she said, a little less emphatically than before.

"Oh yes. Inside," he said as he followed her. He knew he had offended her. So what? Julian trudged up the white granite steps, regally appointed with intricate cast iron banisters comprised of roses intertwined with *fleur de lis*. He stopped behind Sissy as she fiddled with the door knob. Once she entered, the sparkle of the knob caught his eye. Following the gleam, his focus came to rest on it, finding it embossed as a flower. "Hmm."

"What's that, Charlie Boy?"

"The flower on the doorknob. A peony."

She smiled, remembering his mother's glorious reign. "Your Mama loved peonies, even more than roses, I'se suspect. They surrounded the whole place at one time. She particularly favored the pink ones and the white ones, too. But she didn't care for them mixed together," she said, becoming lost in the past somewhat, pondering the strange fact. "You'se would thank she would like the mixed one. She didn't hate it, just never cared to have 'em around." Sissy stared off into space, lost for a moment. "Hmph. Well, let's get you inside and settled, Charlie Boy," she said, returning indoors.

Charlie Boy. He had forgotten the name. At least he believed he had. Now, she had addressed him by his boyhood nickname at least three times in less than five minutes.

"Charlie, it's too hot out there. C'mon in this house, boy!"

Julian tried to cross the threshold, but his feet wouldn't move. His head spun, taking it all in, suddenly transported back to his childhood. "I'd forgotten."

"What? What did you say?" Sissy stood before him, bewildered. Julian didn't look well to her. "Charlie, what's wrong wit' you?"

He didn't hear her speaking to him, lost, engulfed by the past. He remembered, his eyes absorbing it all: the winding staircase, the Baccarat crystal chandelier, the mahogany woodwork, the ornate baroque plastered ceilings, the cornices and moldings, the museum quality antique furnishings. In the center of the floor lay a huge mosaic relief of a pink peony. An unknown force triggered him to look upward.

"Mamère!"

"Mamère? Boy what? Oh." Following his gaze, she found his stare riveted to the life-size painting of Josephine, spanning a large portion of the stairwell wall just beneath the second floor window. "Child, doncha remember that painting? It hung there before you'se was born," Sissy said with a twisted brow, trying to remember. "Well, maybes you don't. I could've sworn that picture was there when you'se was small. 'Member, one of your mamère's friends, who was it now? Oh yeah, Mis'sur Cheval painted it. Doncha remember us tellin' you the story?"

There, in its gold gilded frame, hung a portrait of his mother posing as either Venus de Milo or Eve in the Garden of Eden. A few peonies her only covering, the artist had placed the flowers strategically to conceal her. In the background of the pastoral scene stood a man, perhaps Adam, longing for his Venus or Eve, desiring her, but knowing he could never possess her. In the surrounding garden, many of the peonies were in full bloom, while others budded, awaiting their appointed time of glory upon the earth. Still others had faded, having lost their petals.

"I thought Monpère had destroyed it. He hated it so," he said, trying to sort out the details of his suppressed past.

"Naw. Your mamère just took it down and put it in the attic."

Julian removed his handkerchief from his pocket and swabbed his brow. He could feel the perspiration streaming down his body, beneath his suit. "Why did you bring it down again?"

"I didn't. Lela did. Ask her for yourself after you'se gets settled in. I'll call Theo to take your bags to your room," Sissy said, suddenly noticing the absence of his luggage.

"Oh, I'm not staying. I have a room at the Monteleone."

"I thought you'd checked out?"

"No."

Sissy pursed her lips as she looked him up and down. Deciding not to chastise him, she held her silence. "Well, I'll take you to see Lela, and then you'se can be on your way."

They began their slow ascent up the winding, cantilevered staircase. Julian still found it all to be beautiful, the ceiling plastered with motifs of peonies and angels. His mamère had always believed white peonies covered heaven. Looking up to the third-floor landing, he noticed a section of the plaster adorning its edge didn't match. He turned away.

SISSY EASED THE door open. "Ma'Dame, guess who's here?" She peeked into the darkened room. Sissy stepped aside, granting him entrance.

"Who's there?"

No, this weak, raspy voice couldn't be the same voice, the same woman who had put the fear of God in him, he lamented. "Grandmère, it's me."

"Julian? Is that you, darling?" Life returned to the room.

"Oui, Grandmère. C'est moi!" Rushing to the bed, Julian collapsed atop her, weeping bitterly. She was so old and frail now. What had happened to her? Had it truly been that long?

"*Oui, mon fils.* It's been just that long," Lela said.

Julian stared at her, astounded. He didn't believe he'd verbalized his thought.

"Time has no immediate effect on the young, but it's unkind to the elderly," Lela said. "I'm an old lady now. I was already old when you were born. I was a little younger when your monpère brought your mamère to me."

Julian suppressed his tears, clinging to her, taking care not to crush her frail body. "Grandmère, I'm sorry; for all of it," Julian said in a murmur.

"Well, you should be. But I understand. I wouldn't have returned either, if I had been you. I wasn't sure if you would come now, but the Lord told me you would seek me out before I died. Why the Lord would keep his promise to me is beyond my understanding, but I guess the Good Lord loves me too," she said, laughing to herself, filled with sadness. "The Lord cared for prostitutes so much he saw fit for Rahab to become the grandmère of Jesus, long before David was born."

"Grandmère!"

Lela laughed at his sudden bout of piety. "It's true. Read your Bible. It is written in the Book of Joshua."

Julian couldn't believe his grandmère would blaspheme against the Lord. Not that he was religious, because he wasn't. He couldn't remember the last time he'd attended

Mass. But for the love of God, he would never call Jesus' ancestor a whore. Then again, he had never read the Bible. He didn't care to read the massive book anyway. Who cared?

Listening to his thoughts, Lela winced at his callousness. She struggled to sit up in bed. "Are you hungry, darling? I can have Mario prepare something for you."

"Grandmère, there is no need for concern. I ate at the hotel before coming here."

"Hotel? Where are you staying?"

Julian sighed, bracing himself for her response. "I'm at the Monteleone."

She glared at him.

"Grandmère, I'm tired. I wish to get an early start to-morrow. I just wanted to check in on you and to say hello," he said, anxious to wrap up the unpleasant visit.

"Oh, I see." Lela lamented her great-grandson's cold heart. Well, understandably so. Not many children could witness what he had and remain the same. Julian reminded her of her father. He had shut down upon witnessing the sins of his mother. "Well, you've seen I'm alive. I'm old, and if the Good Lord wills, I will die soon. *Au revoir, mon cher.*"

God, why had he come? "Grandmère, I didn't mean to—"

"*Au revoir, Monsieur Julian.*" Lela turned from him and stared at the ceiling.

Julian stood from her bed side, unwilling to engage in her game of emotional blackmail. "Well, okay Grandmère. I'll see you tomorrow, if you're feeling up to a visit." She continued to stare straight ahead, unresponsive.

Julian left her bedroom, closing the door quietly behind him. Standing in the hallway, he held yet another polished brass peony doorknob in his hand. Allowing his eyes to roam, he looked up at the fresco of his mother's pastoral home, somewhere in northern Louisiana. At least, he had always believed it to be.

Following the brass chain suspended from the ceiling, his eyes rested upon the Baccarat chandelier hanging in the stairwell. Gazing into one of its twinkling crystals, Julian could see the reflection of his mother, Madame Josephine Roussard Chamberie in her prime, demurely smiling down on all who entered the house, in the full blossom of her beauty, youth and favor. She dominated everyone who walked through the doors, but somehow, they never truly realized it. All were simply grateful to be in her presence.

His thoughts skidded forward through the years to his mother's final days. She had loved his father to the point of her own destruction.

"Robert, he's lying! HE'S LYING!"

Julian placed his hands over his ears, attempting to bar the sounds of that night ringing in his head. The door slammed. Car tires screeched. Her body crashed to the floor, echoing in the silence of his heart, like a sack of sugar tossed on the grocer's storeroom floor.

"I gotta go." Julian bolted down the hallway. Descending the stairs, he feared losing consciousness. His vision tunneled as if in a Warner Brothers cartoon's closing trailer, where the circle shrinks smaller and smaller around Porky Pig.

Almost out

"Julian, where are you going?"

He ripped open the front door, escaping to freedom. Stumbling down the steps, he crossed the front lawn, staggering as if drunk. He fell, disoriented. Suddenly, he felt a hand on his shoulder.

Crazed, he whipped around, blinded by fear, his reality colliding with the horrors of his childhood. "Don't touch me!" Julian lay on the lawn with clinched fists, prepared to pummel anyone who attempted to prevent his escape from the house of horrors.

"Julian! Mon fils, what is it with you?"

As the present reclaimed him, he focused on the person who stood before him. "Tante Isabel, I should've never returned here. I'm going to the hotel. I'll check out on Thursday prior to the closing. Call me when, well— Call me once everyone has vacated the house. I'll return to auction off its contents," he said while fighting the urge to hyperventilate.

Isabel fell to her knees and engulfed him in her arms, forcing him to receive her love. "Julian, you cannot run forever. You must face Lela, your parents, and this house. Once you understand what has happened, how and why it all happened, you will be free. You were just a boy, mon fils. You don't know or understand—"

"I AM FREE!" Julian shouted at her, screaming like a lunatic. "I understand what happened here. There's nothing else to know."

"No, you don't." She searched his eyes, navigating the waves of pain and sorrow. "Regard yourself!" Isabel's French accent grew thicker as she became more animated. "You run from here like a madman. You appear as if you will have a heart attack. *Mon cher,* regard yourself!"

Slowly, his breathing normalized as the panic subsided. His clothing felt wet, as if he had just sprinted one hundred miles. He didn't work up such a sweat at the gym. He couldn't breathe. He felt as if he needed an inhaler, but then he remembered he didn't have asthma. "Maybe you're right," he said, conceding.

"I am correct." She removed her handkerchief from her apron pocket and wiped away his tears, as she had done so many times when he was a boy. "Now, return to the hotel and rest. Make your decisions in the morning. Oui, mon cher?"

"Oui, Tante," Julian said.

Chapter 2

Julian plopped down on the bed in his suite. Grandmère looked old and would probably die soon. However, she hadn't changed. People never really did. He just couldn't stay in that house. More determined than ever, he fortified his will to sell the house and to place his grandmère in a nursing home. He had to get her away from all of the pain. She would be much happier there. Once liberated from caring for her, Isabel, Suzette, Sissy and Theo would be free to live their lives.

He never wished to be in his grandmère's position. He didn't want his family to ever feel obligated to care for him. Well, that wasn't exactly true. He didn't wish to fall prey to their schemes to usurp his fortune. If married, maybe his wife would want him dead and then run off with her new lover, fucking on his dime. She would probably stick him in the cheap, state run nursing home where the doctors would slowly medicate him to death. He growled, thinking of every scenario leading to his demise.

He calmed himself, realizing Jannette wasn't quite that devious. She seemed to love him just because. Yeah, right. Although he didn't believe Jannette would mistreat him, one could never be sure. Julian laughed as he turned on the television, admitting he already considered her as his wife. He frowned, for he wasn't sure if she would marry him. How could she not want a handsome man such as himself? All Black women desired a pale Black man like him with curly black hair, an extraordinary physique and chiseled good looks. Not only that, he was well educated and wealthy. However, Jannette didn't seem to care. It didn't matter. She had to marry him and she would. The choice wasn't hers, but his. She would do as she was told.

Grabbing the remote control from the sofa table, Julian flipped through the channels, searching for the telecast of the *March on Washington for Jobs and Freedom*. His anger resurfaced, mad he wasn't there. He calmed himself, finally finding the broadcast. As he surveyed the demonstrators disembarking buses from around the nation, he felt a pang of regret in his heart. He should have and could have attended. His fucking family always seemed to screw up his life.

The station broadcasted interviews from prominent members of American society attending the event. He even viewed a brief interview of A. Philip Randolph, the president of the Brotherhood of Pullman Sleeping Car Porters.

Julian learned he'd been a major champion for the event. He had always believed it had been Reverend King's idea. The telecast provided shots of Bob Dylan along with Peter, Paul, and Mary. The camera zoomed in on Harry Belafonte, Sidney Poitier, and Charleston Heston. Charleston Heston surprised him.

Julian boiled with anger. He could have made a ton of connections at the *March*, but there was nothing he could do about it now. His attention drifted from the telecast back to his 'problem' in New Orleans. He had to figure out what to do with his great-grandmother.

Julian left the bed to make a drink and then sat on the sofa to watch the telecast. Perhaps the hired help was using Grandmère for her money, hoping for a big payday upon her death. One could never trust people. His work in the Civil Rights movement had solidified his convictions. Reverends King and Abernathy had so many enemies, masquerading as committed volunteers to the movement, while working to undermine it at the same time.

Bored, frustrated, and unable to determine a satisfactory outlet for his angst, Julian picked up the telephone to call Jannette. The phone continued to ring. What was she doing?

Each time the phone rang, his agitation grew. Where was the housekeeper? She never left the house except for church on Sunday and to visit her mother on Wednesdays. Julian gritted his teeth. The better question: *Who* was Jannette doing? His anger spiked, ready to call the captain of his jet, ordering him to prepare flight plans for his immediate journey home. He calmed himself as the phone rang.

They had met at Howard University in Washington, D.C., during his graduate studies. Jannette was only a freshman at the time. He fell in love with her the moment he saw her bathing in the evening surf at Martha's Vineyard. God, that yellow bikini with red polka dots! How could such a tiny suit constrain so much tits and ass? Julian laughed, remembering. He needed a cold shower.

His lust mutated into rage once he recalled Jannette's roommate stranding her at the beach. Jealous bitch. Jannette hadn't realized her 'friends' had deserted her until a racist motherfucker harassed her on the beach. She looked around desperately for them to back her up, but they were gone. Julian ran to her defense, wishing to kill the man, running him off. Julian drove her back to campus and they'd been together ever since.

Although their relationship had been a turbulent one, they were still together, somewhat. He felt as if she wished to leave him. She even told him as much during one of their heated arguments. He'd never struck her, or she him, but he refused to back down and neither would she.

Jannette accused Julian of being unloving and intolerant.

He accused her of clandestine behavior. He acknowledged he never accepted her word on anything, but with good reason. Women couldn't be trusted. He always found some guy sniffing around her. However, she always claimed them only to be a friend. But in a strange sense, he trusted and loved her. The phone stopped ringing.

"Hello?"

"Hey, baby."

"Hi, honey. How's your grandmother?"

He could hear her smiling, if that was even possible. Maybe he'd misjudged her. "Old, but she's fine," Julian said. "She's mad at me, though."

"Why is that?"

"Because I refuse to stay in her whorehouse tonight."

Jannette didn't reply.

"Hello? Are you there?"

"Yes," she said.

"What's wrong?"

"You won't stay in the house with your great-grandmother?"

"No," he said.

"See, that's the shit I'm talking about Julian."

"What, Jannette?" She could never be on his side of any issue.

"You're the most unforgiving and inconsiderate soul I've

ever met. She's probably one hundred years old, but you can't tolerate her for an evening?"

"You don't understand—" Julian began.

"You're right, because you won't explain it. So, you're right. I don't. But I do know one thing. If you can't have compassion for your great-grandmother, you'll never have any for me," she said, seething with anger. "I have to go." Jannette slammed the phone on its receiver.

He hung up the phone. Julian just couldn't understand women. To be honest, he couldn't relate to anyone. People tolerated so much bull from one another. One minute they hated each another and the next minute they were friends again. It seemed as if no matter what atrocities people committed against each other, sooner or later, they would reconcile. Now both Grandmère and Jannette were pissed at him because he refused to submit to their emotional torture. He reclined on the sofa, allowing his attention to drift back to the broadcast.

You know Charlie, everyone who loves you, no matter what,

lives in this house.

I know.

Never forget it.

The sun set below the tree line.

Julian's eyes popped open, looking about the room, disoriented. "Mamère." He could still smell her perfume, or at least he imagined he could. He must have dozed off while watching the *March* on TV.

"Damn."

SUZETTE RETURNED TO Lela's room, where she found her propped up in bed and staring out the window. Her mistress was out of sorts. She wasn't sure how to comfort her. At times, one couldn't provide comfort to another, as she had learned throughout her years of service to Lela. In those instances, she had learned to stand in silence while supporting Lela through the repeated fires which had flared up throughout her lifetime.

"Sometimes I wonder if I, well if we, made the correct decision concerning Julian, Suzette," Lela said, perceiving her presence in the room.

"Madame, it was for the best."

"Was it? Look at him! He's tormented. Just tormented!" Lela wiped away her tears. "I thought he would have a chance to live a life of some normalcy with Robert. But look at him. He's so detached. Yet at the same time, he's emotionally raw." She rested her head in her hands. "We should have never sent him away."

Suzette stood at her bedside in silence, unable to determine how to comfort her, all the time knowing she couldn't. She sighed. "Madame, are you hungry?"

Lela didn't hear her inquiry. "They were all so adamant, but now I'm left to deal with him. They're all dead."

"Madame, you cannot change it. What is done is done."

"But it's still not right. Julian isn't right," Lela said, staring out the window. "He's dead inside."

"Ma'Dame?"

Distracted by concern for her grandson, Lela realized someone had addressed her. "Oh! Yes, Sissy darling?"

Opening the door, she peeked inside. "You'se got company."

Suzette and Lela turned one to the other, wondering who it could be. Sissy opened the door wide, allowing the visitor to enter. Tears sprung into Lela's eyes.

"Grandmère, if you don't mind, may I stay here with you this evening?"

Lela began to cry. "Darling, this is your home," Lela said. Finding her strength, Lela threw her legs over the side of the bed. Suzette grabbed her arm, assisting her with standing on her own for the first time in at least three months. Slowly she stood, a little wobbly, but managing. Lela walked over to Julian, kissing him on both cheeks. "Welcome home, darling!"

Chapter 3

New Orleans, Louisiana. August 28, 1963

Lela awoke early the next morning, smiling. Peering outside her window, she found two little red birds sitting on the sill, playfully pecking at one another. Once the birds noticed her watching them, they flew away. "Suzette, come in for a moment, *s'il vous plait*," she called on the intercom.

"*Oui, Madame.*" Suzette appeared at her bedside seconds later.

Lela couldn't contain her joy, overwhelmed with the blessing of her great-grandson's return. She clasped her hands together with glee, and then smiled at her friend. "Suzette, I think I'd like to wear my canary yellow Chanel suit today. Oh, and get my diamond brooch out of the safe, the Cartier one that— Well, my favorite. The one Jamie gave to me."

"Oui, Madame." Suzette permitted a sly smile to course

across her face, encouraging her pale, white complexion to warm, glowing rosy pink. Lela hadn't displayed this much spunk in years. Diamonds? Chanel? Perhaps she'd enjoy her mistress for a few years more after all. Julian's return had done wonders for her spirit. He had given her the will to live again.

WITHIN AN HOUR, Lela had dressed. She sighed as she entered the solarium because she had a taste for Nancy's Eggs Benedict. Mario was a good chef, but not as accomplished as Nancy.

Sissy pulled out the wrought iron upholstered chair for Lela to sit. Lela smiled, thanking her. Sissy filled her glass with water, kissed her on the cheek, and returned indoors.

Lela watched as she left, her eyes filling with tears. Sissy still looked good after so many years. Lela could remember the day they'd sent for her on LaMette's recommendation. LaMette had been her first girl in her 'house.' In fact, LaMette had taught her the art of prostitution and how to be a 'Madam.' It all seemed to have occurred a lifetime ago, but at the same time, it felt as if only a few years had passed.

Had it really been so long? Josephine hired Sissy as her maid once she became pregnant with Julian. Twenty-four years. Lela wiped away her tears. A dove landed on the arm rest of her chair and sang to her for a short time, then flew away. She strengthened herself.

She caressed the brooch, one of the first Cartier pieces Jamie had commissioned for her, a ruby and emerald rose resting upon a sunburst of yellow baguette diamonds of varying hues, encircled with emeralds. The ensemble had been set atop a bramble of golden thorny vines.

Lela considered how empty her life had become without Nancy; well, without all of them. She slipped away, gazing into the Spirit, finding them all standing beside her, encouraging and strengthening her. A gentle breeze passed by. She looked in the direction of the vision once more, finding them all gone.

She fiddled with her locket. Startled, Lela looked up to find Julian standing before her.

"Good morning, Grandmère."

"Bonjour, mon fils," she said as Julian bent over to kiss her.

"Wow, you look great, Grandmère." She really did. Yesterday she appeared as if she required life support. Today she looked as if she planned to lunch at the club.

"Thank you, darling."

As he sat at the breakfast table, Julian considered her. In the light of day, she didn't look a day over sixty years old. Then he reasoned she had lived a life of immense wealth and ease. Why shouldn't she look good?

"Darling, is that what you believe?" Lela raised an eyebrow.

"What?"

"Do you believe I've lived a life of ease? Is that what you really think?"

Julian stared at her with his mouth gapped open. "I never said that Grandmère."

"Darling, you didn't have to. One gains certain gifts at this age," she said, snickering. "Life has been far from easy for me. You don't know anything about me or this family."

Oh shit, he thought. Now I must hear about how she had to hoe the back forty acres as a child.

"No, darling. I was never a field hand, although there were many days I wished I had been. Life was hard for me with my father. He desired to love me, but instead he chose to hate me because I wasn't White," she said. "Do you know your great-great-grandpère's name?"

"No."

"Augustus Chevalier."

"Augustus Chevalier?" During his undergraduate years at Morehouse College, Julian had enrolled in a course on antebellum Louisiana. In his studies, the professor had discussed the large Louisiana land owners, primarily because they were large slaveholders. He remembered the name Chevalier. "No, it can't be—"

"Yes darling, it's true. I'm the daughter of Augustus Chevalier, one of the largest slaveholders in Floridian Louisiana. We still own the land and the house. A few years after you left, I refurbished the plantation. I don't know why, because I had suffered so much misery there. Nevertheless, I had to do it because the land is a part of me." She sipped her *cafe au lait*. "I hope to turn it into a museum one day, so the younger generations might understand what it was like to be a slave."

Lela nodded, validating in her heart the work she had done to revitalize the land. "I managed to save the slave cabins as well, even the little white house where Maman and I had once lived, next to the mansion. I did that about ten years after I returned to New Orleans from Paris during the 1910's. It was so run down. It seemed as if only yesterday I had dreamed of escaping that house and its miseries."

Julian sat before her with his mouth open.

"Aren't you hungry, darling? Your breakfast is getting cold."

Julian shook off his shock and resumed eating. Lela focused on the misted goblet, skating through time, harnessing scenes of the most poignant and defining moments of her early years popping up to the surface of her spirit. "Augustus killed my sister Lily, well, my half-sister, in his mission to kill me. I loved her so much, and she loved me too. Father hated her because he never believed her to be his child, treating her like, well, like a bastard child. There's no such thing you know, as a bastard. If God hadn't intended for the child to be, it would never have been."

Julian couldn't eat, entranced with her story.

"I didn't have another sister until Elise. We were separated for thirty years after I left Paris in the 1890's. She believed me to be dead."

Julian couldn't address all of the loose ends. "Wait, slow down, Grandmère," he said, gulping down his eggs. "You had a sister named Elise?"

"Well, technically we were best friends; but, we were just as close, if not closer, than Lily and me."

"Oh. Where did you meet and what happened to her?"

Clasping her hands together, Lela smiled, giddy with the remembrance of the times they had enjoyed together. "We met in Paris. We had so much fun together! We could talk about anything and never worry about one betraying the confidence of the other. In the 1920's, she discovered I was alive, for she believed me to be dead due to my unexplained disappearance from Parisian society. I visited her in Paris shortly thereafter, and then she came here to stay with me during World War II."

"Oh!" Julian remembered a White lady staying with them when he was very little. She always gave him candy, hugs and love. "Auntie Leelee? Is that Elise?" Lela smiled and nodded. "I remember her!" Julian hadn't thought of her in years. How could he have forgotten her? He felt a little bad, but he got over it. "So why were you in Paris?"

"Jamie and I lived there for many years." Lela felt a twinge in her heart, mentioning his name.

Julian picked up the misted crystal goblet, taking a sip. "Who's Jamie?"

"My husband."

He spat out his water. "Your husband? You were married?"

"Goodness yes! James Roberts was my husband. We loved each other with all of our hearts," she said, surprised he didn't know. But then again, why would he? She had not used her married name since leaving France in 1890.

"James Roberts?" Julian's mind raced, conducting an internal scan of every course he had taken in college. "I read about a James Roberts in one of my grad courses at Howard. He invested heavily in a variety of Union industries during the Civil War."

"Oui. That's him, *probablement*." Lela smiled, full of whimsy, lost in the heyday and joy of her life. "He'd loved me since my St. Helena days. He was *bon ami* of Jean Charles." Lela sipped her café au lait.

"Hey, wasn't he White?"

Lela pondered his question for a moment. "Yes, I believe

he was, if my memory hasn't failed me."

Julian sat before her, astounded. "Grandmère, if you have that type of money, which must be worth billions by now, why were you all— Well you and Mamère—"

"Why did we operate a house of ill-repute?" Lela dabbed the corners of her mouth with the linen hem-stitched napkin. "Darling, life's road is never smooth. It's always bumpy, but it evens out in the end, making us stronger for the journey."

"I don't understand," Julian said.

"Darling, life is gray. Nothing is ever as it should be, as we dream. Nothing is either right or wrong. It just is, and we must walk the path we're given, that we choose." She paused, thinking. "It was neither my dream nor my choice to become a Madam. But now, your mamère was a different story. Josephine had an ax to grind and she couldn't be happy until she had beheaded everyone around her."

Julian frowned and returned to his breakfast without a response to her comment.

Considering him as he finished his meal, Lela admired her magnificent great-grandson. She knew at that moment she'd made the right decision regarding his future ten years before, her fears of the previous evening subsiding. He had turned out well; however, a void remained inside of him. She couldn't determine how to fix it. A rage lurked just beneath the surface, which could potentially threaten his fullness as a man, obstructing his destiny.

She could see her Josephine in him. God he looked like her. There was a hint of Robert, especially in his nose, mouth, and coloring, but then again, Josephine and Robert always did favor one another. But who she really saw was her Jamie. Her eyes welled up with tears.

Julian placed his fork and napkin on his plate, having devoured his breakfast. He noticed her distress. "Grandmère, what's wrong?"

"Nothing," she said, sniffling. "You remind me your great-grandfather." She dabbed her eyes with the napkin, which she would never do under normal circumstances, but she didn't have a handkerchief nearby. "You're nearly the spitting image of him."

"Do you have any pictures of him?"

"Yes. I will show them to you."

Against his will, Julian couldn't help but feel compassion for his grandmère, repeatedly enduring the loss of her husband from so long ago, over and over again. "You loved him very much, didn't you, Grandmère?"

"Yes darling, with all of my heart." Lela said, remembering. "Even then, Jamie knew me. He recognized me, seeing me for who I am long before I ever knew." She became lost, finally understanding it all, after so many decades. She observed her love in the Spirit, cuddling a beautiful rose in his hands, careful not to harm its petals.

A sob escaped her, a vision of Jamie materializing before her. "He tried— He tried so hard to protect his Rose, but it wasn't to be. He maintained his obedience to *notre Dieu*, having the strength of heart to allow God's will to be," she said to herself, seeing the truth for the first time after seventy-three years. "My God! He knew and submitted, fooling all of us." Until that moment, she had no idea he'd known. He hid it all so well, experiencing life so happy-go-lucky. She could now see his sight had exceeded all of theirs.

"Grandmère, what are you speaking of?"

Lela continued to search the Spirit for understanding. The vision had closed. "Never mind, darling. One day, you will see it too. But not for many years."

Julian frowned, accepting his grandmère's senility.

She ignored his thoughts. "Although it's been close to eighty years, it seems as if he just left me today." Lela took control of her emotions. She didn't wish to mourn the past, but to save the future. Lela depressed the intercom button. "Isabel, darling?"

A few moments later, she appeared. "Yes, Maman?"

"Bring the book, please."

Isabel disappeared into the house, returning a few moments later with a beautiful leather-bound book, tanned to a reddish brown. Embossed upon its cover was the title, *La Rose Family History*, along with a beautiful flower, a rose with many layers of petals. Julian kept his negative comments to himself, waiting for her to explain.

"This, my son, is your family history," she said with a proud smile, patting the book. "I began to write this book the day you left with Robert. I had always dreamed you'd return here before I died, to talk to me. God has answered my prayers." She handed him the book.

Tenuously he opened it. Flipping through, he stopped at a page with a list of names.

Ette

Masufa

Camille Chevalier

Sammie

Emeline Roberts

Sarah the Slave

Lily and Lela Chevalier

Cindy Fairmont Chevalier

Samantha Roberts

Josephine Puryear Roussard Chamberie

In another column, she listed the men, parallel to the women.

Anon

Nat

Emmanuel Chevalier

Augustus Chevalier

Michael Roberts

Teddy (Theodore Bailey)

Jean Charles Chevalier

James Roberts

Humphrey Puryear

Robert Chamberie

Julian Charles Chamberie.

Then he noticed a column designated as 'Adversaries.'

Augustus Chevalier

Michael and Emmie Sue Roberts

Josef and Hanzel Johannesen

Anton Lemont and Chantelle Marie Trouvier

Anthony and Michael Buonoguidi

Jonas Purvis

Sylvester Thomas

"Grandmère, why did you include 'Adversaries' as members of our family history?"

"Because they are. Without these persons, neither would we have become the family nor individuals we are today. These souls tested our character."

He sighed, saying nothing as he continued reading. 'Spirit Relations.'

Barachiel

Raguel

Sealtiel

Jonathan Chamberie

Comtesse Elise Micheaux

Monsieur Toussaint Bailey

Allen Pruett

Theo Wilson

Isabel Mitchell Lee

Suzette Demain

Nancy and Nate Johnson

William Johnson

Marion Clemens

Claude Hicks

Benito Salvatorie

Stanley "Stank" Ingalls

Peter O'Bannion

"Grandmère, are these people related to us?"

"Yes darling they are, but, not as you understand. Spirits are bonded to one another in ways understood only by God. Love is stronger than any bond that blood invokes. It's the strongest tie and the deadliest too. But one must walk the Earth for many years to understand this." She smiled, spotting the beignets. When had they arrive? Isabel must have delivered them with the book. Lela took one from the platter and dove in, dropping powdered sugar all over her suit, which she brushed away. "You may not have learned this as of yet."

Julian considered it all, remembering his childhood. "Nancy and Nate, Theo, especially Uncle Toot; they were all relatives to me in my heart, even though I understood they weren't blood related."

She smiled, nodding.

Julian continued to flip through the book, reviewing the photos and reading her narratives. "Is this your husband?" He regarded a picture of a dapper man with a handle bar mustache. Lela nodded with tears flowing from her eyes. He studied the picture, unable to detect any resemblance, concealed by his huge mustache. He then remembered the man wasn't his blood relative, anyway.

Hearing his thoughts, Lela gawked at him, but said nothing.

"Why are you giving this to me?"

"You should be aware of your blood, as well as your spirit relations," Lela said, pondering all she wished to reveal to him about the lives, the trials and the triumphs of their family members, in spite of their adversaries' best efforts to destroy them in his mission to thwart the family's forward progression into their destiny. With much effort, she retreated from the scenes of the past, not wishing to bombard Julian with tales he had no desire to either know or understand. She would have to take an indirect route to her intended destination.

Lela changed the subject, deciding to have a little fun with her great-grandson. "Mon cher, how old do you believe me to be?"

Julian threw up his hands, laughing. "Oh, I'm not answering that question."

Lela laughed, patting his hand. "I won't be angry. Tell me."

Julian studied her as one considering betting on a horse. "God, Grandmère. What, eighty-five years old? I can't really tell. You could be in your sixties if I didn't know better. However, based on how old Mamère would've been, I would have to say you must be much older."

Lela blushed filled with coyness, as if a young girl before her first suitor. "I was born in 1847. I was born a slave."

"That's impossible. That means that you're—"

"One hundred sixteen years old. Yes, darling. It's true," she said, smiling.

"That's impossible! You can still walk. You're not senile. Heck, if I liked older women, I might even ask you out."

Lela laughed. "Oh, you are the flatterer, just like your great-grandpère."

"Are you sure, Grandmère? Maybe they told you the wrong date."

Lela popped the last delicious morsel of her beignet into her mouth. She considered having another, but decided she would wait. She couldn't understand why she was so hungry. Oh, yes. She had not eaten for the past three months, fasting in anticipation of Julian's arrival. "No, it's well documented. I was born February 12, 1847. My father, Augustus, kept impeccable records regarding his slaves, since they were his investments. Augustus had heard the Union troops were coming to his plantation, La Rose. So, he forced Toussaint to help him hide his valuables. However, the soldiers never came, and Augustus made no haste in retrieving his possessions." Her countenance darkened. "Augustus died unexpectedly in 1875. Upon his death, Toussaint dug up the gold and used it to purchase the property in New Orleans for his mortuary. He hid the books in his stable for a number of years."

Lela sighed, nodded, and then refocused on the topic at hand. "Anyhow, he showed me the ledger many years later, recording the date of my birth. I was eight pounds, seven ounces."

"Unbelievable. Researchers would kill for that kind of documentation."

"I know." She'd forgotten her point, determining it to be unimportant. "Well, I'm sure this ancient history is tiring, so I won't bore you. I just wished for you to have documentation of where you come from."

Julian grunted a bit and stared at the book. He caressed the heavy vellum between his fingers. A spirit crept into him, causing him to shiver. He stopped turning the pages once he came to a photo of himself, Mamère and Monpère in Brussels, in some sort of palace. A man stood in the background. Julian suppressed his urge to cry.

Mamère was so beautiful and happy, as was Monpère. Julian noticed himself smiling broadly as well. He clutched something in his hand. He remembered. "That man standing behind Monpère had given me a golden coin. He said it was my cameo on the coin!" Julian looked to his grandmother. She said nothing, watching him.

Curiosity, more so sentiment and admiration, mounted within his heart. "Grandmère, will you tell me the story?"

Lela's eyes lit up. *I win,* her heart sung into the Spirit. She danced upon the throne of the Most High, while Lucifer and Mammon scowled, watching her. She didn't care. *He asked of his own volition and interest,* she said to them. The Adversary frowned, but she could see he would never surrender. Lucifer and Mammon departed the Throne of the Most High in defeat.

Julian belonged to her.

Lela returned her attention to her great-grandson. "Darling, the story is very long. I'm sure you must have other things to attend to, such as the sale of this house and finding somewhere for me to live," she said.

Julian scowled, brushing her comments aside. "Well, I have some time today. If you're not busy, maybe you could help me understand—"

"Why your mamère died?"

"Yes," he said, unwilling to release his emotions and hurt. A teardrop fell on his mother's image in the photo album. He wiped it away, but it had already stained the picture. Julian closed the book and placed it on the table.

"I'm not sure if I can. Only Josephine could explain it." She watched as disappointment claimed him. "But perhaps I can explain to you how Josephine became the person she came to be."

"That would be great, Grandmère," Julian said.

Unable to contain her joy, Lela barely managed to conceal her victorious smile from Julian and the heavens above. "Well, allow us go indoors where we can be comfortable."

"If you don't mind, may we sit on the terrace? It's cool this morning. Maybe we can sit on the swing, as we did when I was little," Julian said, once again a little boy in need of his grandmother's love and protection.

Lela smiled, watching as his heart emerge from its darkness. "Yes, darling. We can do that."

Julian assisted his grandmère to the swing built for two

under the huge live oak tree. Once he found her to be set-tled, he ran back to the house and asked Isabel to bring out a bottle of Grandmère's favorite brandy along with some Glenlivet for him.

Returning to the swing, he sat down and rocked it. After a few moments, he laid his head on her shoulder, resting in her comfort. Without warning, they found themselves in a timeless place without troubles, a place where only reflection and understanding were allowed. They swayed in the breeze of the New Orleans morning for some time.

"Grandmère, what happened to Mamère?" His throat contracted with emotion, but he suppressed it. "Why did she have to die? Was I that bad?"

"Darling, of course not!" Lela patted him and sighed. "I must start at the beginning. You may be here for a while."

He closed his eyes, snuggling into her breast. He ingest-ed her perfume. Chanel 22? He hadn't smelled the fragrance since his mamère died. "I have time, Grandmère."

She smiled as she released the tension of the morning and wandered back through the decades. Lela stared at the rose bush. She could sense the plant's anxious anticipation of her consent and command. *Bloom*, Lela whispered to it in her mind. Without warning, the awaiting buds of the bush blossomed, unveiling its glory to the world.

From the corner of his eye, Julian perceived a movement

in the bush. He turned his gaze in the direction of the movement, shocked to find the dormant rose bush in full bloom, parading its blossoms for the world to see. Its scent filled the garden, relaxing him. Julian then turned to his grandmère, finding her gaze locked on the bush. He wished to question her, but said nothing.

Lela sighed. "I'm not sure what to tell you about your great-great-grandpère. I'm not sure how to explain his ways to you, Julian," she said, engrossed in a time passed.

"Who?"

She winced, consumed. "My Father." Lela returned her focus to him, barely connected with the present. She looked up to the heavens. Lela wished to avoid the revelation. She fiddled with Julian's fingers as she considered her path. Julian wished to hear about his mother. Maybe she should just tell him about her. But she knew it would do him little good to learn about his mother alone. Once he gained a feeling, a passion for his family, then he would be able to receive Josephine for whom she was. At the same time, she knew he could never love anyone unconditionally, not even his own mother. Lela closed her eyes and smiled a bit. Yes, perhaps it would help.

Lela stroked Julian's hair as she peered into the past. Although different, she found Julian to be the same as he'd always been. She sighed, still gripped by the internal struggle regarding whether she should tell him or not. How could she not tell him? Augustus had impacted all their lives, usually with cataclysmic results. Yet, she didn't wish to stunt Julian's spiritual development with the recollection. *I won't tell him very much. I'll allow him to sort it all out within his soul,* she decided in her heart.

"My father loved me. He loved us, meaning my mother and me. He loved us both without prejudice, at least for a time."

PART II

Chapter 1

Lela

I believe somewhere in his twisted heart, my father loved my mother. Looking back, I think the illegality of their relationship frustrated him. He was a racist; do not misunderstand me. He hated 'Niggers' and never failed to exercise his hatred for our race and for every race of man, other than his own.

I don't think I ever heard him address anyone without the use of a slur. Now that I think about it, the only group he didn't insult was the French, his own race. His kinsmen were simply referred to as assholes, bastards, motherfuckers, so on. If he liked someone, which was rare, he would address them with respect.

Over the years, his cruelty against his slaves reached insurmountable heights. However, for some unexplainable reason, he loved Maman. For some strange reason he found her beautiful, and she was. Isabel favors Maman a great deal.

In fact, Isabel could be Maman. I believe Maman was a bit taller than my petite Issy.

She was the darkest brown, her skin appearing as the most luxurious velvet. In fact, I had purchased a dark brown sable coat for your mother prior to her first tour of Paris. When I saw her in the coat, I thought of Maman, the deep rich color of the fur reminding me of her intrinsic beauty.

When Augustus returned to the plantation from boarding school in New Orleans, his mother Camille was all but dead, dying of insanity. The old folks said Augustus' father, Emmanuel, had killed her lover and imprisoned her in her bedroom. After her lover's execution, Camille's sanity steadily slipped away. She had become a frail, old woman once Augustus returned home.

La Rose Plantation. St. Helena's Parish, Louisiana. 1818

EMMANUEL STEPPED OUT onto the shaded colonnade and looked down the hill leading to the house. After a few moments, he spotted the carriage rounding the bend, as it began its ascent up the steep hill. His heart beat fast with the anticipation of seeing his little Gus, now a man.

"Yo' chap done finally come home, mon Frère."

Emmanuel smiled, happy that no one was around. They could be themselves. "Oui, mon Frère Lawrence. He has."

Lawrence dropped his persona as a slave and returned to his natural form, enjoying the moment. He stretched his wings and smiled. "He's a whip, mon Frère," he said. "I love him, but at the same time, I can't endure him." Lawrence sighed. "But I suppose I will. I have for centuries. I can endure him for another fifty or sixty years."

Emmanuel patted him on the shoulder and lit a cigarette. "I suppose you might, Lawrence."

The men watched as the carriage eased to a stop before the house. Lawrence concealed himself and sighed, detecting a spirit of tyranny. "May our Lord, the Holy One Jesus, help us, mon Frère." Lawrence returned to his appointed role as a slave, adorning the demeanor and dialect once more.

Emmanuel sighed. Hatred radiated from the carriage. "Our Lord has always protected us, mon Frère, since the beginning."

Lawrence descended the steps, calling for the boys to come and help with the young master's luggage. "Bienvenue, Massa' Augustus!"

He ignored Lawrence, stepping from the carriage and walking past him.

Emmanuel admired his son. Although disagreeable, he had grown into a handsome young man. He admired his suit of clothes and accoutrements. He had instructed Manny, his tailor, to leave France for a short while and open a shop in

New Orleans. Of course, his son had gravitated to the shop without any prompting or direction from him. Good taste and style were an innate trait within his genes. Emmanuel smiled at his son as he walked up the stairs. "Augustus."

Augustus sneered at his father, still angry he'd been forced to return. "Bonjour, Papa."

Emmanuel tenuously hugged his son. He could feel his son's repulsion, wishing not to be touched. Emmanuel ignored him, overjoyed to have him back. The boy had to be at least six feet tall, towering over him. How could he grow so tall? Emmanuel was merely five feet, six inches tall. While gracing the court of Versailles, he wore his man heels, propelling him to five feet nine inches tall. Perhaps he had inherited his height from his mother.

He reached up and removed his son's hat so he could muss his curly black locks. When Augustus was a child, Emmanuel presumed he would grow out of the curls. He never did. Maybe he'd inherited the curly hair from his mother as well. "How was your journey?"

"As pleasant as traveling through the swamp in June can be, Papa."

Emmanuel sighed. "Augustus, it's time for you to learn how to manage the plantation."

Augustus glared at his father, ignoring his admonishment. "Where is Maman?"

Emmanuel had hoped he wouldn't inquire about her. But then again, why would he not? "Son, she isn't well today."

"Well, who would expect her to be? I take it she's in her room?" Augustus pushed by him.

Emmanuel's joy melted into heartbreak. His son hated him for what had happened to his mother. Emmanuel couldn't deny his role in her demise. He wiped the tears from his eyes. He had ruined his son.

AUGUSTUS ENTERED THE house, running up the stairs. Stopping before her door, he braced himself. After a few moments, he eased the door opened.

This cannot be her. The words echoed through his mind, now a vacuum. Who was this old woman in the bed? Taking a closer look he recognized her, detecting her latent beauty. However, her beauty had succumbed to heartbreak and insanity. Augustus suppressed his tears. He couldn't understand why he felt anything for this woman. She had destroyed their family. Well, he had destroyed his family by telling his father of a matter which didn't concern him. "Maman?"

Camille continued to stare into a land only she could see, rocking while patting her right elbow. Her hair was white, well what was left of it. He could see her scalp. Augustus touched her lightly.

"Stop, Emmanuel! Don't! Do not—"

"Maman, I'm Augustus."

Camille attempted to focus. "Gus?" Visiting the realm of the living for the first time in eight years, Camille began to cry. "*Mon bèbè*." She wept, touching his face, his hair, amazed her dream sat beside her. "*Vous etes l'homme maintenant!* Where is my little boy?" She clutched his face in her hands as she kissed him.

Augustus quelled his emotions, stroking his mother's thin, wispy hair.

"God has answered my prayers. Now, I can die."

"Maman!"

Camille smiled. "I'm sorry, my darling. Maman is sorry." Her face wet, unable to cope with her reality any longer, Camille submitted to the comfort of insanity once again. "Maman loves you. I never meant to hurt you. I loved him too. But, how could I forget you?" Camille's crazed eyes focused on her son once more. "What caused me to believe I loved him more than you? You were my life. How could I forget that?" Camille wept, her heart full of bitterness.

"Oh God!" Camille rocked fiercely, and then her face softened as her rocking leveled off to an easy pace. A queer smile overtook her as her eyes blanked out, escaping the reality of her actions and her life.

Augustus ran from the room and down the stairs. He bumped into something.

"I'se sorry, Mis'sur."

Augustus' red eyes saw what blocked his passage. He had accidentally looked the slave in the eye. What were slaves? But this one was different. She looked away, running from the stairwell to the rear of the house. Augustus fell back against the wall and wailed for his mother. He slid down, coming to rest on the step.

Lawrence handed him a glass of water.

Augustus accepted it, gulping it down. He placed the glass on the stair and closed his eyes. "I've killed her." He took another gulp of water, swallowing his rage and guilt. "I will never love again," he said, taking comfort in the realm of detachment.

He opened his eyes to find himself alone. Arising from the stair step, Augustus completed his descent, stopping for a moment in the coolness of the foyer. He left the house to take a walk.

THE SLAVES WATCHED him without looking at him. He could feel their collective, inquisitive silence as he walked through the slave quarters. It had the ambiance of a small town. His father owned over 300 hundred slaves. Augustus sneered. The slaves seemed to live better than St. Helena Parish's poor White trash.

The slaves had set up little stalls where they bartered

their goods with each other. He'd noticed, before his driver had turned onto the private, winding road leading up to the plantation, little shops on his father's property along the main road. He was sure the shops were operated by the slaves. He remembered seeing a dressmaker, tailor, weaver and dye house, blacksmith, gun maker, grocer, *chocolatier*, *patisserie*, and a butcher. Knowing his father, he probably paid the slaves a small percentage of the profits. Augustus frowned. Once he took over, he planned to discontinue the slaves' cut. They were slaves. What did they need with money? They belonged to him.

Augustus removed his jacket. He'd become hot and thirsty. "There must be a pump around here somewhere," he said as he searched the little square. The slaves parted, allowing him passage through the teaming area. He soon found a well near the water troughs for the animals. As he approached, he spotted a slave woman cranking the handle. Once the bucket reached the top, she removed it and poured the contents into another bucket.

"Give me some water."

The woman turned to him from her labor and Augustus eyes lighted. It was the slave girl from the house.

"Oui, Mis'sur." She ran into the little shed and brought out a porcelain cup. She poured water into it and handed it to Augustus.

"Have Niggers been drinking out of this cup?"

"No Mis'sur. This here's Mis'sur's cup. We'se keeps it here for him," she said, looking down.

Augustus admired her. She was different than any woman he'd ever met, Nigger or White. "What's your name, gal?"

"Sammie."

Lela

Maman told me she could never figure out the look in Father's eyes that day. It was as if he'd just died, but once he saw her, hope returned to his heart. He behaved as if he had received a reprieve of some sort, another chance at life.

He actually courted her. Augustus would give Maman coffee and sugar. He would pick flowers for her and bring them by her cabin. Her mother, Minnie, frowned on the relationship. She would talk to Emmanuel about them, telling him the two couldn't be together.

Emmanuel tried to dissuade his son from taking up with Maman, for it was a sin for them to be together. But, it was too late. He had already slept with Maman.

Maman floated about on a cloud, for she was a young girl in love. Emmanuel and Minnie frowned on their relationship as I told you earlier, but I don't think it was due to race and class. There was another secret reason why they discouraged the union.

I believe Augustus killed my grandmère. I believe he poisoned her. Minnie had convinced Emmanuel to send Augustus away, at least for a short time, so the relationship could cool off. I guess Emmanuel had talked to Augustus about a long trip to France to check on the family's château.

Maman had told me that soon after the discussion, Augustus brought some candy to Minnie as a peace offering. Minnie had a sweet tooth, Emmanuel having spoiled her with treats over the years. I wonder about the relationship between Emmanuel and Minnie, especially after my grandfather Nat died. Well actually, he'd disappeared and no one ever found his body. Maman told me Grandmère grieved for some time, but then Emmanuel talked to and comforted her. Soon after, the two took up together.

I'm getting away from the story. Maman wanted a piece of candy too, but Augustus whisked her away, telling her she could have some later. Maman told me when Minnie ate that candy, she was fine. The other slaves spotted her throughout the day, going about her chores. She went to bed that night, perfectly fine.

The next morning, Maman couldn't wake her mother.

I can't prove it, but I know in my heart he poisoned her. Once Minnie died, Maman said one of the slaves spotted Augustus and Emmanuel arguing on the other side of the slave quarters. Then, two other men appeared out of nowhere and grabbed Emmanuel, one Negro and the other with slanted eyes (I'm assuming he was Asian, but the slaves had never seen a person from the East before, so this was the description provided). They led him away. Many of the slaves believed the men had murdered Emmanuel. Augustus never really seemed concerned about his father's fate. Once his father disappeared, Augustus became master of the plantation. He had his father declared legally dead soon after his disappearance.

NOW WITH BOTH Minnie and Emmanuel gone, Augustus became more brazen in his relationship with Maman. The slave community raised a collective eyebrow, but said nothing. Emmanuel had favored both Maman and her mother, Minnie. It had been rumored that Emmanuel was Maman's father, and not Nat. But she looked so much like Nat and Minnie, the rumor didn't live long.

Maman was dark, like midnight. She was beautiful. She had tight curled hair, which she allowed to grow long. She parted her hair down the middle. She'd told me as a child that her sister, Sarah, would come once a week to plait her hair in two braids, which coursed down her neck. By the end of the week, the tightly curled hairs would have liberated themselves from the braids, giving her hair a fuzzy appearance. I guess your generation, Julian, would call her hair kinky or nappy. I guess we called it nappy hair too.

Maman had big eyes with a nose to match. She had the most beautiful nose, large, but well formed, complementing her delicate face. She had the loveliest lips, large, appearing as if Michelangelo had painted them upon a canvas, over-sized for the times, but perfectly shaped.

Anyhow, now with both Minnie and Emmanuel gone, the slave community shunned Maman. She had no other but her sisters, the butler, Lawrence, and of course, Augustus. The women would laugh and point at her, calling her Li'l Massa's whore. One even spat on her, but she would never reveal the woman's identity.

Chapter 2

La Rose Plantation. 1820

Having finished scrubbing the large wooden table, Sammie returned to the galvanized washtub and wrung out her rag. It had been a long day and she was tired. As she worked, her thoughts drifted to Gus. She loved him and she knew he loved her too. She wished she had someone to talk to. Now that her mother was dead, she felt alone at times.

Her sisters had nothing but bad things to say about him, telling her Augustus was only using her, that he had other women. She didn't believe them, well wouldn't allow herself to do so. Sallie and Sylvia would go on and on, telling her what they'd overheard from the other slave women. Sarah stood by in silence, saying nothing. It concerned Sammie that Sarah had nothing to say. She always had something to say.

Her sisters told her Augustus had fathered children with

these women as well. "Sammie, he's the Massa'," Sylvia said. "What, you'se thanks he's gonna marry you? Well, let me tell you something, he ain't. You'se just a Nigger on his land, his slave." Having finished nursing her daughter, little Nancy, Sylvia placed her on the floor. All of the women watched her. The child grabbed her mother's leg and hoisted herself up, wobbling. Nancy steadied herself and looked to each aunt, smiling and gurgling. A long slobber escaped her single tooth grin. Her gaze coming to rest on her Aunt Sammie's sad countenance, she stumbled over to her without falling, walking about six feet. The women cried and cheered. "She ain't even one!" Sylvia wept with pride.

Sammie picked the child up, kissed and hugged her. "You'se a smart, strong, li'l ole gal, ain't yah?" Sammie said in a low voice for only Nancy to hear. "You'se gonna help my gal one day, ain't yah?"

Little Nancy laughed, the joy returning to her face. Sammie returned her to the floor. She took a couple of steps, but soon returned to her knees. Once she tired herself out, she plopped down on her rump, ready to listen to the debate.

Sammie became sad once more. How could her sisters not be happy for her? She suppressed her tears.

Sallie ran to her side and embraced her. She could see her sisters had hurt Sammie's feelings. "Sylvia, she just a child! She's too young to know no bettah!" Sallie guided Sammie to the kitchen bench and sat beside her. "Baby, Sylvia just doesn't know how to put thangs nice, but she's telling you'se the truth. Doncha go gittin' mix up wit' him."

Sammie nodded and walked away, hiding her tears from her sisters.

SAMMIE HUNG THE last pot on the rack suspended from the ceiling, pushing the conversation from earlier that day from her mind. "They'se don't knows him like I'se do."

"You're right. They don't."

Augustus grabbed her behind and she jumped. She hadn't heard him enter the kitchen. Turning her towards him, he allowed his hands to caress her newly formed hips. "I made these." He led her out the back door to her house.

Once Augustus had finished and fallen asleep beside her, she recalled the pain of their first encounter. She had bled quite a bit. It was so big and it didn't fit, but somehow he got it in. Augustus appeared to have been ignited by her suffering and the blood. He had said, "Now I know you're mine. I'm you're first and your last. You can't go with no one else but me, ever." She thought she'd heard him whisper he loved her. She didn't question him, but stored the belief away in her heart. Although they had been together ever since the last harvest, it still hurt to be with him, but the pain had become less severe.

"YOU'SE A LIAR!" Lawrence tried to restrain Sammie, but she broke free and charged Augustus. Forgetting who he was, she now only saw the man who had betrayed her. She tried to strike him, but Lawrence grabbed her. "You'se cain't do it. You'se cain't!"

Augustus closed his heart and mind to Sammie's tirade. "They belong to me Sammie. They're my property. Don't interfere in my business."

Trader Jans placed collars on the necks of Sylvia and Sallie. He shackled their feet and their hands, and then loaded them into the wagon, one chained to the other. Although their eyes were red, they didn't allow a tear to fall. Yet, they couldn't speak either, knowing they wouldn't be able to suppress their sorrow.

Baby Nancy wailed in Sylvia's arms. Barely able to move due to the chains and the collar, Sylvia comforted the child to the best of her ability, attempting to soothe her baby's wails.

Sammie continued to struggle in Lawrence's arms, shouting curses at Augustus, cursing his family and his seed. Augustus wouldn't look at her. "Here are their deeds. Get them out of here." Jans tipped his hat to Augustus, climbed into the wagon and drove away.

Sammie continued to scream for her niece and her sisters. She broke away from Lawrence and ran after the wagon. Sallie turned around on the bench as the wagon picked up speed. "Go back, Sammie. Doncha runs after us none. This is where's you'se belong, not us." Sallie turned her back to her sister as the wagon sped off, carrying them away to an uncertain future.

Sammie lay in the road and wailed for her sisters. After some time, she felt a hand grab her wrist and yank her up from where she lay. She despised him. She kicked Augustus and ran off, hiding in the woods.

SHE'D NEVER BELIEVED he would do it, although Sarah had told her he would. Cold and afraid, Sammie hid in the brush. The sounds of the night terrified her. She feared a snake would bite her, or a wild animal would attack and kill her. She should have climbed up in a tree, but someone might have spotted her. She wondered if they were searching for her. She lay on a pile of leaves and sleep claimed her.

The song of the birds awoke her. She got up and brushed herself off, noticing insect bites on her leg. They itched. She walked a short distance from her pallet of leaves and found a place to relieve herself.

Her stomach churned. She couldn't remember if she'd eaten anything the day before. Searching about, she found a patch of wild strawberries. She devoured all of them whether ripe or not. She walked through the woods searching for water. She found a small pool of water and drank from it. She was satisfied.

As the heat of the day came upon her, she returned to her little palette finding it infested with ants. No wonder she was covered in bites. She returned to the pool of water. Her stomach began to ache and cramp. Doubled over in pain, Sammie found a private place. She hoisted her skirts and relieved herself.

Sammie began to sweat, chills over taking her. "That water was bad," she said to herself as she stumbled through the woods. After several hours, she collapsed.

"Wake up, baby."

The sky now dark with only the moon to illuminate it, Sammie opened her eyes. She gazed at the stars, each parading their glory upon the evening stage. She felt something cold on her forehead and sat up.

"Lie still, Sammie."

She didn't see anyone at first. She turned her head from the left and then to the right. Turning to the left once more, Sammie found her sister Sarah at her side. "Whatcha doin' here?"

Sarah the Slave smiled as she walked over to the fire she'd

built. "To sees 'bout you." Removing the kettle, she poured the liquid into a tin cup. "Drank this." Sammie obeyed and ingested the foul liquid. She lay back down and slept.

It was still dark when she awoke. She could see Sarah sitting on a log, smoking her corn cob pipe. Sarah turned to her. "How's you'se feeling?"

"I'm better." Sammie sat up on the palette.

"Whatcha doin' out in these woods, gal? You'se don't know nothin' 'bout survivin' out here."

Sammie began to cry, wiping the rebellious tears from her eyes. "I ain't going back," she said. "How could you let him sells them?"

"They don't belong to me. I'se couldn't stop Augustus." Sarah sat beside her sister on the palette. "They'se alright, honey. Augustus done sold Sallie to a place out near Covington. He sent Sylvia somewhere up north in Mississippi."

Sammie stared at her sister in horror. She had never heard of the place. Although she believed she would see Sallie from time to time, she knew she would never see Sylvia again. She hated him.

"Hate kills the soul," Sarah said. "You should know that from hangin' out wit' your boyfriend." Sarah patted her sister's hand and gave her some bread and water. Sammie ate it. "It's time for you'se to go back, honey."

"I'se ain't never going back, Sarah."

"Well, where's you gonna go?"

Sammie considered her options. "Maybe's I'se can lives out here, wit' you."

Sarah laughed. "Gal, you ain't been gone a day before you ate some poison berries and drank some bad water." She could see the hurt in her sister's eyes, so Sarah suppressed her laughter. "Look gal, you'se the baby. You'se got a special purpose in this life and you ain't gonna find it out here in these woods. Go back."

"He's gonna beat me."

Sarah stared at her sister as if the most foolish woman in the world. She didn't understand the power she held over her master. "He ain't gonna do nothin' to you, trust me on this, Sammie. You'se the only one on God's Earth he won't hurt." Looking into the future Sarah grimaced, but she held her tongue. "Go home."

Early in the morning before daylight, Sammie approached the cabin. She smelled coffee. She opened the door to her cabin to find a hot pot on the hearth, the embers glowing beneath, casting a dim glow within the room. "I had to sell them."

Stricken with fear, Sammie froze in horror as Augustus struck a match and lit the candle. He approached her from the darkened corner of the room. Setting the candle hold-er on the table, he took Sammie in his arms and stroked her arms lightly. "I don't want nobody turning you against me. You're all I got. I can't have nobody filling your head with strange notions." Sammie, still paralyzed with fear, said nothing. "They're going be alright, Sammie. They're in a good place. I just couldn't take the chance."

"What chance, Gus? They ain't done nothin' to you!" Sammie's rage trumped her fear, blurting out her true thoughts.

He kissed her. She resisted him at first, but succumbed. "You don't need nobody but me, Sammie. You're mine. You don't need them, only me." Augustus led her to the small bed and lay her down.

SAMMIE HAD INHERITED Minnie's clothes and had begun wearing the garments. She gathered strength and comfort from them. Her mother had left her two skirts, one petticoat, two blouses, two dresses (one for Sunday Meeting), and four aprons. What slave possessed so many clothes? But her mother had. Her mother's wardrobe made her feel like an adult, no longer adorning the shift dresses of her childhood. Now, she dressed as a woman, although Gus had told her she'd been a woman after the first time they did it together.

Her finger tips fondled the three coffee beans in her

apron pocket. She loved coffee and Augustus always brought her some when he came to call. Once, he handed her the three beans. "Keep these. I want you to think of me when you see them." She always carried them with her.

She now knew he'd messed around with other women in the Quarter. She remembered the first time she found out about one of them from her sisters. She'd avoided him after that for a time, always leaving the kitchen before he would come for her in the evening. He let her be for a while. Then one night he came in and made her do business with him. "Don't make me force you," he had told her. She submitted to him. After it was done, he patted her behind. "I fuck them, but I love you. You'll always be mine, gal." After that night, his dealings with the other women went underground, as if he wished to shield his encounters from her.

She didn't have any friends. The other women seemed to hate her, although she had been nothing but kind and friendly. Once in a while, her sister Sarah would visit her, telling her about the children Augustus had fathered with the other women. Then she would pat her knee and tell her not to concern herself with it too much.

Having decided on the menu for the day, Sammie set out to gather the ingredients. She'd decided to bake a ham for Gus, his favorite dish. He never told her as much, but she had noticed he always enjoyed seconds and thirds.

Sammie pulled up the kitchen door and began her journey to the smoke house, located in the square. The birds fluttered from branch to branch, criss-crossing the path she traveled. They sang a beautiful song, welcoming the day.

Entering the square, she watched as her neighbors went about the business of the day. It was Sunday, so the square was crowded since no one had to work in the fields. It was the one day of rest the slave community enjoyed each week.

Sammie placed her hand in her skirt pockets. She fiddled with the coffee beans as she cut across the square to the smokehouse. "Mornin' ya'll," she said to the ladies standing near the well. They didn't respond. She bowed her head a bit and entered the smoke house.

Exiting a short time later with the ham slung over her shoulder, she found the ladies still standing at the well. "Ya'll have a good day."

"You too," Li'l Sis said, but then stifled her greeting.

"What I'se tell you'se 'bout Li'l Massa's whore?" Liddy said before everyone present. "She's ain't your friend. She ain't none of our friend. He sold off her blood but she's still fuckin' him."

Sammie stood before them, humiliated and ashamed. She wanted to cry, but held her hurt. Liddy was right. How could she continue to be with him after he'd sold off her sisters? But what could she do, tell him no? Sammie lowered her head and walked away. She felt something warm and wet on her neck. Reflexively, she wiped away the clear fluid. She turned around.

"Git from 'round here," Liddy said. Sammie rushed away as she heard the women chattering behind her.

Sammie barely made it to her cabin, her eyes flooded with tears. She burst into the door and slammed it shut behind her. "I'se shouldda told her 'bout herself," she said as she rebuilt the fire. Usually, she didn't build a fire in the middle of the day, since she was at the big house. Yet, her mind was scattered, thinking of Liddy and Li'l Sis. They were right. She was just Gus's whore and she knew it. What would her sisters think if they knew she had continued to sleep with the man who had sold them off? But what choice did she have?

Sammie sat in the chair and wept. She'd suffered nothing but heartache since her mother's death. If her mother had been alive, none of this would have happened.

"What's wrong with you, gal?"

Sammie jumped in her chair. "Where did you come from, Sarah?"

"Whatcha mean?"

"You'se wasn't here a second ago."

Sarah sat on the floor at her feet. "I'se heard you'se cryin' and could sees that you'se was upset, so I'se came to see 'bout you."

Sammie nodded. "How do you appear like that, outta nowhere?" She rubbed her red, swollen eyes. "I'se don't mean no disrespect, but do you do's that voodoo they talks about?"

Sarah smiled and patted her sister's knee. "Naw, that ain't it, honey. I'se just takes after our daddy."

She didn't wish to play games with her sister. She hadn't seen her for some time. "You'se ain't always here, is you?"

Sarah smiled at her sister. "No."

Sammie chewed her fingernail, trying to figure out what to ask her sister. "You'se ain't a woman, is you?"

"Why you'se askin'?"

"You'se can moves around. You'se don't seem to be bound by folks."

Sarah kneeled before her sister. She took her hand and patted it. "I'se a woman. I'se just takes after our father, likes I'se said before."

Sammie pondered her sister's words. She always believed her to be Minnie's daughter. "You'se Nat's daughter?"

Sarah stared at her in disbelief. She could see she didn't know. "Naw. Nat ain't my daddy, but we have the same daddy."

Sammie wondered how they both could have the same daddy if Nat wasn't her daddy. Sarah wasn't making sense.

Sarah smoothed down her sister's hair. She needed to re-braid it. Sammie never could braid her own hair. "I'se takes after my daddy. I'se inherited his ability to move around, different from normal folks. I'se can see likes he do's too. But I'se ain't Nat's daughter."

"Is you Minnie's daughter?" Sammie asked.

"Naw, my mama died when she was birthin' me. You'se don't know her."

"Oh." Confusion racked Sammie's brain. "But you'se ain't Nat's daughter?"

"Naw," Sarah said.

"But I'se am…" Sammie couldn't make sense of it all.

Sarah said nothing. "What's wrong, Sammie?"

Sammie twisted the folds of her mother's skirt between her fingers. "Folks talkin' 'bout me.

Sarah twisted her face in judgment.

Seeing the rage on her sister's face, Sammie downplayed her anguish, yet tears flowed from her eyes against her will. "It ain't nothin'."

"Yes, it is. Tell me."

Sammie sobbed, releasing the hurt and pain. After a time, the pain subsided. "They'se sayin' I'se a whore." Sammie broke down in grief again. "And they'se right."

"Why you'se say that?"

"Nothin' but a whore would fucks the man who sold off her kin." Sammie arose from her chair and left the cabin to go and prepare supper for Augustus. Once she returned, she found her cabin empty. She crawled into bed. Gus didn't come to see her that night. She wept until the rooster crowed the following morning.

Augustus rolled off of her, exhausted. He hadn't experienced a release of such magnitude in months. He put his arm around her waist, laying his head on her breast. His hand sauntered downward, savoring the warm wetness between her legs. He kissed her.

Sammie tried to smile. She turned her head away, hiding her tears. *Dirty.*

"What's wrong with you?" His euphoria mutated into irritation.

"Nothin'."

He sighed. Sleep claimed him.

She couldn't stand the whispers and the snickering. Sammie looked around the square of the slave quarters. She watched as folks milled about, socializing and trading. It had been over a week since she had last visited the square. The first people she spotted were Liddy and Li'l Sis holding their wicker laundry baskets near the well with their friends. They cut their eyes in her direction and laughed, returning to their conversation.

Sammie lowered her head and entered the butcher shop. Lance had her order ready. She gathered it and left the shop, walking away quickly, ashamed.

AUGUSTUS MOUNTED HIS black stallion. He had finally named the animal, after owning him for three months. He called him Rock. When the breeder brought the animal to La Rose, Augustus fell in love with the creature. The sunlight skimmed across the animal's jet-black hair, possessing the luster and gleam of polished silver. The prominence of his rump and the muscles of his hind quarters left no question in Augustus' mind the animal could run fast. The animal flaunted his fabulous tail, fanning it about himself majestically. The horse knew he was beautiful. Augustus was sold. The breeder told him the price and Augustus handed him the gold. He didn't even haggle with him.

Bored with being at home, Augustus decided to ride out to the fields to see what the slaves were doing. His new overseer was too soft on them. He wished to instill a little fear in the overseer's heart.

Sarah the Slave appeared before Rock. The animal reared

back, nearly throwing Augustus. "What the fuck is your problem, Niggah?"

Sarah smiled. "I'se ain't got the problem. Sammie does."

He knew she must want something for her to show herself. Sarah was the one slave on the plantation he couldn't harness and control. At times, he found he feared her. She was a witch with the powers to appear and disappear at will. Sarah did as she pleased and he couldn't stop her. She never worked in the fields. He couldn't force her either because he could never catch her. "What's her problem?"

"Folks givin' her a hard time."

Augustus frowned, his face flushing hot with fury. "About what?"

"'Bout you, 'Massa.'" She placed her corn cob pipe in her mouth and lit it. She exhaled, the smoke entering Rock's nostrils.

The horse reared back again; Augustus struggled to maintain control. Augustus got the animal to settle down after a few minutes. "Say what you mean, woman!"

Augustus' jaw dropped as she told him the story, learning that two of the slave women had been spreading rumors about him and Sammie, discussing how loud they fucked, how she sucked his dick. His face flushed red once Sarah told him they had branded her whore for fucking the man who had sold off her sisters.

Sammie had never said anything to him about her life with the other slaves. Frankly, he didn't care. But who would have the balls to shun her? He knew the other slaves knew about them, but this? He wondered why she hadn't ever said anything.

"What could she say?" Sarah responded to his thoughts. "She's yo' property. She has to obey you and lives with them. So, she just suffers."

Augustus frowned. "Who else knows about it?"

"I'se reckon everybody in the parish by now. Folks talk. I'se sure it's done spread to the other plantations. Some of the house slaves with good relations with their Massa's may have mentioned it to them."

No longer in the mood for a ride, Augustus turned Rock around and returned to the house. Since his father's departure, the slaves had grown lax. Once Sammie's mother died, the slaves had allowed their collective hatred for her daughter to shine. Jealous bitches. Minnie had been the slave queen on the plantation with everyone, Black and White, bowing to her. He never understood the phenomenon. Now with both Minnie and Emmanuel gone, the slaves behaved as they wished.

Leaving Rock to graze on the lawn, he walked up the stairs to the house. Usually he would have yelled for the stable boy to come and get the animal, but Sammie's suffering and the slaves' lack of fear of him consumed his thoughts. Who would have the guts to speak against him? He didn't beat them enough, that was for sure. He had been too concerned with fucking Sammie over the years.

He stood before the front door, recalling one of his rare visits to the plantation while a teenager. He'd overheard Lawrence and his father talking to a Chinaman and a Nigger in the kitchen one day. He had never seen a Chinaman before. The Nigger was different, for he dressed in a strange garb, as if royalty, a king. He had to be seven feet tall, for his legs stretched for miles while sitting in the kitchen chair.

The men didn't see him as they continued their discussion on what to do about Minnie's enemies. His father said, "He will handle it." The men nodded in consensus. Everyone stopped talking once Augustus entered the kitchen.

Augustus sighed, banishing the irrelevant memory from his mind, returning to the matter at hand. The slaves didn't live in a proper state of fear. His father had ruined them. They only saw Augustus as 'Li'l Massa.'

Lawrence opened the door for him. "What have you heard?" Augustus asked him as he entered the house.

"'Bout what, Mis'sur?"

"Don't play with me," Augustus said, growling at him.

Lawrence sighed. He couldn't lie. "It's true."

Augustus' anger spiked. "Do you know these bitches

who are running down my Sammie?"

Lawrence smiled. Even slavery and Augustus' hatred of Negroes couldn't suppress his love for her. Sammie's soul had been created especially for their evil one. Only she had ever been able to manage him throughout the ages. "Yessah. I'se reckon I'se do."

Augustus went to his library. Lawrence followed him.

WITHIN DAYS, AUGUSTUS had ferreted out the identities of the primary culprits fueling gossip about Sammie: Liddy and Li'l Sis. About one month later, Augustus sent Sammie and Sarah to visit their sister Sallie on the Roberts plantation. The women were excited about the excursion, for they hadn't seen their sister since Augustus had sold her off years before. Sarah didn't even question Augustus about his sudden act of generosity, much to his relief.

Once their wagon pulled away, he mounted Rock and rode south to the far side of the plantation. He'd ordered the overseer to pull the slaves out of the fields and gather them at the appointed place. Rounding the bend, he spotted a group of about five hundred dusty slaves. He stopped once he reached the bank of the Tangipahoa River, which flowed through a large portion of his property of 2,500 acres.

He'd hired and armed some poor White trash from town, at least two hundred, who sat perched in the trees, as well as patrolling the crowd on foot, to provide security for the day's events. The horrified slave community stared in disbelief at their friends and neighbors, Liddy and Li'l Sis, each tied spread eagle to 'x' shaped crosses planted in the marshy ground. The women had been missing for some time. Some believed the two had run off, but it didn't make sense, for they had left their children behind. Now the slaves understood why. They were surprised to find them alive, having survived the heat of an unknown number of days in the sun.

The slave men sported rebellion in their eyes, trying to figure out a way to ambush Augustus and free the women. They had heard stories of his cruelty. But with all of the guards, the slave men stood their ground, angry and powerless to do anything to help the women.

Augustus stood before his property, his skin reddened by his rage, more so than the merciless sun. "Look here, Niggers," Augustus began, "...ya'll gonna learn about keeping me and my business out of your mouths." They all stared at the ground, refusing to make eye contact with him. Some of the women dropped to their knees, bewailing God to help them. "Get up. God can't help you." Terrified, the women returned to their feet.

"I own you and run everything on this here place. Ya'll don't run shit. I do!" His yelling dislodged leaves from the trees. "If I hear one more word about my business, I'll do the same to you that I'm about to do to them. Let me hear one word.

"And if ya'll think ya'll gonna exile some of my Niggah's because of what they do for me, ya'll got another thang coming," he said, looking at Liddy's and Li'l Sis' compatriots, standing with the slave community. They should have been grateful they weren't mounted on crosses next to their friends.

Augustus walked over to a small table, where a knife lay in its sheath. His friend, Jim Bowie, had sent it to him as a gift a few years before. He had always fantasized about using it on Sarah the Slave, but these two would do.

"Open their mouths."

The slave men, dubbed as the 'Sheddahs by the other slaves, approached the women. They worked in the Shed, as the slaves called it, named for the façade which concealed the entrance to Augustus' underground torture chamber. Augustus had begun to train his torturers and executioners at an early age, eradicating their souls and consciences. They didn't fraternize with the other slaves.

The men forced the women to open their mouths with ease. They placed a metal guard inside of each of them, constructed for the purpose of preventing their mouths from closing.

Augustus felt prickly, overcome with anticipation.

He walked to the first woman, Liddy, and whispered, "You won't ever say another muttering word against my Sammie, bitch. You understand me?" She glared at him, unafraid. He could see in her eyes her hatred for Sammie. Augustus reached in, pulled out her tongue and sliced it off at the base. The slaves watching screamed in terror. Liddy's mother, Bits, went into hysterics. She charged Augustus, but one of the slave men caught her and carried her away. Augustus laughed as he watched blood spray from Liddy's mouth to the dusty earth, the drops creating little clouds upon landing. Li'l Sis squirmed on her cross beside her friend, screaming and trying to escape.

Augustus continued to laugh, throwing the woman's tongue out near the bank of the river. A buzzard swooped down from a tree, picked it up, and flew away to enjoy his treat. There was a fluttering in the trees. Augustus looked up to find them full of buzzards, awaiting their supper.

Augustus repeated the process with the second woman. However, it wasn't the same for him. She was just a follower. Dumb Nigger. However, she'd been condemned to suffer the same fate as her friend. One of the slave women observing the grisly punishment passed out.

Once Augustus had cut out the tongues of the women, the Sheddahs busied themselves with arranging wood at the base of each cross. They returned to their places and stood at attention after they'd finished, staring into the crowd with blank, empty eyes.

Augustus lit the kindling beneath the feet of the women. As the flames grew stronger, he piled more wood on the fire, until it soared up into the late afternoon sky. After a time, the women stopped screaming, consumed. He hadn't believed one could scream without a tongue. He closed his eyes and relaxed, now having executed his judgment. He remembered the slaves. "Go back to the fields."

They turned to leave, one at a time, traumatized and humiliated, each dreaming of escaping their horrible existence. "Don't ya'll forget!" Augustus called to them as they wandered away, crestfallen. "And I don't want to hear no talk about this, either."

Chapter 3

New Orleans, Louisiana. August 28, 1963

Julian sat before his grandmère, dumbfounded. Why would she claim a man like Augustus? Her story reaffirmed his passion for the Civil Rights Movement. The time had come for Blacks to free themselves from the cruelty and the racism which they had suffered in America for centuries.

He leaned back in the swing, finding he didn't completely hate Augustus for what he had done. God help anyone who ever spoke against his Jannette. But in Augustus' case, his love for his slave wasn't the only motivator. He wanted the slaves to fear him.

Julian frowned, his ethics, morals, and beliefs in racial equality colliding into one irresolvable tangle with his need for control and revenge. He hated Augustus, but at the same time, he couldn't confess with confidence he would have behaved differently.

Lela smirked and said nothing, having listened to his internal struggle. "May I have a glass of water please, darling?"

Julian arose from the swing and poured a glass of ice water from the pitcher. Isabel hadn't returned for hours, or so it seemed. How could the ice persevere in such heat? He returned to the swing and presented the cool drink to his grandmother.

"Thank you, darling," she said with a smile. The cold drink soothed and revived her. She could feel the liquid traveling down her esophagus, disappearing from her senses somewhere within her depths. She sat the glass on the table and closed her eyes. Extending her arm, she welcomed her little one into her embrace. She wouldn't be able to endure him upon her breast much longer, for the heat of the day would soon be upon them.

"Augustus had many enemies, for apparent reasons. Not only was he a cruel and violent man, but wealthy as well. Father was savvy when it came to financial matters. Once the Confederacy seceded from the Union, President Davis came to see Father personally, requesting he invest in the rebel nation. Father laughed in his face, telling the President he wouldn't give him gold for worthless paper. The Confederacy wanted to kill him for it, but nothing ever came of it. However, I'm getting away from my story.

"In any case, Father often outwitted people, purchasing

their land in forced sales. He was notorious for extending loans to people with terms he knew they couldn't meet. He would call in the loan at the agreed upon time and evict the owners if they couldn't pay. He would watch the tax rolls and acquire property via tax sales. If there had been such a thing as bullet proof carriages, Father would have needed one."

She turned to her great-grandson, finding him engrossed with every word she'd spoken. "I won't go into any more detail about his business dealings. You seem as if you're taking mental notes."

"I'm just listening to your story, Grandmère," Julian said full of innocence. He batted his eyes. "So, what were some of your father's other business practices?"

Lela laughed. "You believe I've only just met you today, boy. I won't tell you anymore about it. I'm not even sure how I fell onto the subject." Lela grimaced as she tried to remember the point of her story. "Oh yes, Michael Roberts."

"Who?"

"He was your great-great-grandfather's cousin. Some say they were first cousins." Lela laughed to herself. "Hmph. He was your great-great-grandfather too, now that I think about it."

Julian stared at her, waiting for her to continue. "Well anyway, they hated each other with bitterness. I can't really convey to you the level of hatred that persisted between the men. They were always in the mist of some complicated, covert plan to destroy the other. They never succeeded in killing each other, though." Lela's face sagged with sorrow. "But they managed to destroy everyone around them."

La Rose Plantation. 1828

AUGUSTUS HATED HIM. He could remember hitting him on the head with a wooden toy horse when they were eight years old. He couldn't remember what Michael had done to him. In any case, they didn't see each other again until boarding school in New Orleans. Augustus remembered seeing and despising him instantly, even before he knew his name. The two men had tormented one another throughout school.

Lenore. Augustus had dated her during his last few years of boarding school. He'd considered marrying her, but he knew he wouldn't because they had been fucking the whole time. When he entered her for the first time, he'd known she wasn't a virgin. There was no telling whom she'd been with. After he dumped her, she took up with Michael. He discarded her soon after.

No matter how Augustus tried to avoid Michael, somehow he always manifested himself into Augustus' life. Now, he had returned so many years later, bringing his daughter and wife to call. Why couldn't Michael leave him the fuck alone? Augustus knew Michael's recent visits weren't social. He wanted something from him, but Augustus had yet to figure out what he desired.

Michael had even brought along his maid, Sallie, whom Augustus had sold to him years before. The slave despised him and she did little to conceal her hatred. He had a mind to take her out back and cane her. Sammie had screamed and cried when the trader carried her sisters off, but he hadn't cared. His mission had been to rid himself of all her witchy sisters. He didn't want them conjuring spells against him and Sammie. He desired to be the only person to control Sammie. Yet, he owned her. What could anyone do or say to him anyway?

Augustus frowned as he watched Sammie and Sallie walking down the path to the back of the house arm in arm, skipping like children. He left the parlor window and poured himself a drink, listening as Lawrence received his unwanted guests. With drink in hand, he returned to the window in time to see the stable boy take the carriage. His eyes fell to the servant's bench on the rear of the carriage, causing him to think of Sallie again.

He couldn't understand why Michael would bring Sallie along for the visit. Augustus didn't want Michael and his family in his home, let alone his house slaves.

During a previous visit, Michael had explained he wanted Sallie to visit her sisters, Sammie and Sarah. Why would a man like Michael care if his slave visited her relations?

Sammie would often cry to Augustus about how Sallie suffered in Michael's home. He would wonder how Sammie could know what went on there. Then he remembered spooky Sarah. She'd probably told her. Sammie had even tried to convince him to buy Sallie back from Michael. He'd told her no, for he already had chicken foot rubbing Sarah running around the plantation casting spells. She didn't need any help from her sister. Eventually, he caved in. He couldn't stand to see Sammie so sad. But Michael had turned him down, declaring he would never sell her. Augustus accepted his reply, relieved.

Michael's sudden compassion for Sallie convinced Augustus that he was up to something. Although Augustus only interacted with her during the monthly visits, he still hated her. It was as if Sallie could see and hear his thoughts. She was nothing like Sammie; however, she was every bit like Sarah. He had considered selling Sarah off to the East, but he couldn't catch and hold her long enough to do so. Augustus entered the parlor and sat in his chair, consumed by the motives and concealed plots of the women. An irritating sound jolted him from his thoughts.

"Are you listening to me, Augustus?"

"No. I'm trying not to." Dammit, when had Michael and his family even entered the parlor? Augustus frowned, his mind overrun with how to eradicate the remnants of the witch coven from his plantation. Michael, his family and his slave were getting on his nerves.

Michael ignored him. "I said Emmie Sue is doing well in school."

Augustus laughed. "What? She can read? Amazing."

Michael turned red with fury, but then inhaled to curtail his rage. "Why yes, quite well in fact. And guess what? She can count too."

Emeline, Michael's wife, smoothed the child's hair and patted her hand. She hoped Augustus' cruel remarks hadn't hurt her child's feelings. However, Emmie Sue was quite precocious for an eleven year old girl. Emeline could see the fire in her, the passion for life which she had always lacked. "Emmie Sue, why don't you read for Monsieur Chevalier?"

"Did I tell you to speak, Emeline?" Michael said. "Shut your mouth and sit there."

Emeline folded her hands and lowered her head.

"Emmie Sue, go and sit next to Monsieur Chevalier," Michael said.

Augustus nearly choked on his bourbon. "What?"

"I want her to sit beside you, Chevalier. You got a problem with that?"

"Yes! She's a child. Besides, I'm sitting in a chair and there's no room for her."

Deaf to his protests, Emmie Sue stood up from the sofa. Augustus watched the little girl approach him. Stopping before him, she curtsied while gazing into his eyes with a sultry nature unbecoming and unnatural for an eleven-year-old girl. Was she trying to seduce him? She sat on his lap. He could feel her wiggling.

"Are you a whoremonger, Roberts? Get down Emmie Sue and go and sit next to your mother!" Augustus shot up from his chair, tossing the child off his lap.

Emmie Sue landed on the floor; her skirts flared about. Her eyes filled tears, hurt by his rejection. She ran to her father.

"What the hell is wrong with you, Chevalier?"

"I'm fine. The question is what is wrong with you? Are you insane?" Augustus said to Michael. "Get out and take your whores and your Nigger with you. Don't come back."

Michael swept Emmie Sue into his arms from the floor. "Come along, darling," he said to her, cooing and kissing her on the cheek. "Emeline!"

Emeline stood from the sofa. "It was a pleasure to see you again Monsieur—"

Michael slapped her. Emmie Sue scowled at her mother. "What did I tell you about running your mouth, Emeline?"

She bowed her head, following her husband and daughter from the home.

"Sallie!"

Lawrence shook his head. "I'se guess yo' Massa' done worn out his welcome."

"I'se suspect so," Sallie said. Her amusement melted into terror at the thought of returning to her master's plantation. "Lawd I'se wish I could stay here with ya'll," Sallie said, embracing both of her sisters at once.

"Why? Augustus ain't no better," Sarah said. She desired to kill him, but her sister Sammie loved him. In any case, he hadn't fulfilled his purpose. She couldn't touch him. God wouldn't allow her to slay Augustus for a reason she couldn't understand. She guessed the Most High reserved the honor for another she couldn't see.

"But he ain't like Michael. Ya'll don't see how he beats poor Ma'Dame," Sallie said. "He's made that li'l ole wicked Emmie Sue his wife. She treats Ma'Dame just as bad." Sallie eyes welled with emotion. She couldn't share with them the abuse she herself endured. She couldn't think about it, for she was powerless to change her situation. *Her babies.* She banished the thought of them to a surreal dream to be forgotten. "I'se just wishes we could all get away from him."

Lawrence hugged and kissed her, strengthening her.

"One day, ya'll will. I'se promise yah."

"Sallie! Nigger, I said come on," Michael yelled from somewhere outside of the house.

"Today would've been perfect if Sylvia could've been here too," Sallie said, ignoring her master's demands for a moment. They all nodded in agreement, suppressing their emotions.

They walked out the kitchen door, escorting their loved one to the side drive. The driver had pulled the carriage around. Sallie sat on the servant's bench located on the rear of the carriage. Sallie wrapped the straps around her wrists which helped her to hold on during the rough ride to the Roberts plantation. The driver popped his reigns and the horse began his slow strut, pulling them away. Sallie swung her legs beneath the carriage as if on a swing, wishing to present a happy picture to her sisters.

Sarah and Sammie watched her until the carriage turned the bend at the bottom of the hill, leaving their view. "Only the Lawd knows when we'se gonna see her again," Sammie said. She began to weep.

"Well, if the Most High knows, then it's gonna be alright. We'll see her again, I suspects," Sarah said. She walked away. Sammie blinked her eyes. Sarah had vanished, headed for destinations unknown.

Chapter 4

La Rose Plantation. 1828

The witch sisters, along with all of his other slaves, seemed to circumvent Augustus' power on the plantation. He couldn't understand the phenomenon. They reminded him of the witches in Shakespeare's play, *Macbeth*. The women only needed a cauldron to complete their persona.

But as he thought about it more, Sammie didn't seem to have the power of witchcraft at her disposal. She ruled him without magic, and he knew it. Her unexplainable control over him troubled Augustus. Who was this slave woman who held dominion over him? Not that she exercised it, he wasn't even sure if she knew she held the power; however, he knew in his heart he could never deny her.

Augustus puffed on his cigar, considering his slaves. Although he had cut out the tongues and burned alive the gossiping women, he still believed his slaves didn't hold the appropriate level of fear for him. He would watch them at times, roaming the plantation and working it as if they owned it. His father had ruined them.

"You are correct, *mon neveu*. They don't fear you as they should."

Augustus turned in his wing chair, finding an unfamiliar man standing in the doorway of his library. He didn't know him, but he did in a way. "You aren't my uncle. What are you doing here?" Augustus asked as the hairs stood on the back of his neck. "Lawrence let you in?"

The man smiled, remaining in the doorway. "I let myself in. No one stood at the door," he said.

"Who are you?"

"I'm your uncle, Richard Roberts." Augustus raked his memory, but he didn't know him. "I am your Cousin Michael's father. I am Emmanuel's brother," he said. "I regret to say we weren't close."

Considering the asshole he'd fathered, it wasn't difficult to figure out why his papa hadn't brought them around much. Augustus frowned. "Get out."

Richard's face collapsed into a sad droop. "I will do as you've asked," he said "It's a pity really. I've waited many years to meet you, but your father blocked the introduction."

"If he didn't want me to know you, I'm sure there was a reason why. Go," Augustus said as he rose from his chair, headed for the fireplace. His shotgun hung above the mantle. If the intruder wouldn't leave on his own, he would kill him.

"There is no need for violence, mon neveu. I will go. I just wanted to offer you help." Richard stood in the doorway, full of humility. "You are a great deal like me, Augustus. You understand how to set aside emotion and do what is required to prosper. If you chose to accept my gift, you will become the wealthiest landowner in the state, dare I say the country. However the choice is yours."

Augustus considered his words.

Richard could see his 'gift' interested him. "Allow me to help you, Augustus."

"Help me with what?"

"Your problem with your slaves."

Augustus stood before the fireplace with the shotgun in his hands, now interested in what the intruder had to say. "What?"

Richard reached into his breast pocket and removed a yellowed envelope. "This letter contains the key to breaking your slaves for all time. They will be forever subservient to you for generations to come. If you follow the instructions contained within this note, they will never be able to ban together and rise up against you."

Augustus could feel the heat rising within him. He knew

the man spoke the truth. He walked over to him and snatched the ancient note, removing it from its envelope.

Gentlemen,

I greet you here on the bank of the James River in the year of our Lord, one thousand seven hundred and twelve. First I shall thank you, the Gentlemen of the Colony of Virginia, for bringing me here. I am here to help you solve some of your problems with slaves. Your invitation reached me on my modest plantation in the West Indies where I have experimented with some of the newest and still the oldest methods for control of slaves. Ancient Rome would envy us if my program is implemented.

As our boat sailed south on the James River, named for our illustrious King James, whose bible we cherish, I saw enough to know that your program is not unique. While Rome used cords of wood as crosses for standing human bodies along the old highways in great numbers, you are here using the tree and the rope on occasion. I caught the whiff of a dead slave hanging from a tree a couple of miles back. You are not only losing valuable stock by hangings, you are having uprisings, slaves are running away, your crops are sometimes left in the fields too long for maximum profit, you suffer occasional fires, your animals are killed, gentlemen... you know what your problems are; I do not need to elaborate. I am not here to enumerate your problems, I am here to introduce you to a method of solving them.

In my bag here, I have a fool-proof method for controlling your black slaves. I guarantee every one of you that if installed correctly it will control the slaves for at least 300 years. My method is simple, any member of your family or any overseer can use it. I have outlined a number of differences among the slaves, and I take these differences and make them bigger. I use fear, distrust, and envy for control purposes. These methods have worked on my modest plantation in the West Indies, and it will work throughout the South. Take this simple little test of differences and think about them. On the top of my list is "Age", but it is there because it only starts with an "A"; the second is "Color" or shade; there is intelligence, size, sex, size of plantations, attitude of owners, whether the slaves live in the valley, on a hill, East, West, North, South, have fine or coarse hair, or is tall or short. Now that you have a list of differences, I shall give you an outline of action-but before that, I shall assure you that distrust is stronger than trust, and envy is stronger than adulation, respect, or admiration. The Black Slave, after receiving this indoctrination, shall carry on and will become self-refueling and self-generating for hundreds of years, maybe thousands.

Don't forget, you must pitch the old Black versus the young Black male, and the young Black male against the old

Black male. You must use the dark skinned slaves versus the light skinned slaves, and the light skinned slaves versus the dark skinned slaves. You must use the female versus the male, and the male versus the female. You must also have your servants and overseers distrust all Blacks, but it is necessary that your slaves trust and depend on us. They must love, respect, and trust only us.

Gentlemen, these kits are your keys to control, use them. Have your wives and children use them. Never miss opportunity. My plan is guaranteed, and the good thing about this plan is that if used intensely for one year, the slaves themselves will remain perpetually distrustful.

Yours,

Willie Lynch

"Where did you get this?"

Richard removed a bit of lint from the sleeve of his jacket. "Mr. Lynch discussed its principles with me prior to penning it, while still in the West Indies." Richard smirked. "Dare I say that many of the ideas are mine, but I will grant him the glory of it."

Augustus' face corkscrewed into a scowl. *He's a liar, yet he tells the truth.* He considered the man who stood before him. He appeared to be Augustus' age. "This letter was written in 1712. You don't appear to be over one hundred years old."

Richard smoothed down his hair. "I've aged well."

"Hmph!" Augustus replaced the letter in its delicate envelope as he pondered its words. Could it work? It wouldn't take much to institute the letter's recommendations. However, he understood the strength of camaraderie within the slave community on the La Rose Plantation.

"Yes, you're correct when you say the bond is strong here," Richard interjected. "But once the older generation dies, who will be present to counsel and advise the younger generation? Start with them. They are the weaker link."

Augustus nodded. It could work, especially now that Minnie was dead. "Why are you giving this to me?"

Richard backed away from the threshold. Augustus sighed, acknowledging his own lack of hospitality. "Come in. Would you care for a drink?"

Richard smiled broadly and stepped across the threshold. He sat in Augustus' favorite chair. Augustus frowned, but allowed his infringement. "I wished to share this information with your father, but he would never invite me in. He refused to give me audience, accept at his own discretion."

Lawrence ran into the library winded, having run a mile. How hadn't he seen him? He had only left the house for a few moments to pray for a slave who had fallen ill. "Oh Lawd!"

Richard laughed. "You have perfect timing, Nigger,"

Richard said. "Bring me a cup of Darjeeling, no sugar. And make sure it's hot."

Defeated, Lawrence turned to leave.

"And Nigger?"

Lawrence turned to face him, his rage mounting within him. "Yessah?"

"Don't spit in my tea."

Augustus consumed the letter, reading it over and over again. Richard stayed with him at La Rose for almost a year, training Augustus on the letter's principles and practices. Lawrence burned with fury every day over the extended stay of the unwanted visitor.

AUGUSTUS TOURED THE Quarter with Richard. The air of the community had changed. Where the slaves once existed in an *esprit de corps* of unity and liberty, they were now distrustful of one another. The women didn't chat together as much. The men kept to themselves. Only the old timers sat together, looking on their children in despair.

The slaves seemed to trade less with each other, now looking to Augustus to provide their sustenance. Instead of going before the elders to settle disputes with one another, they now brought their grievances to the overseer, who then presented their complaints to Augustus. "Do you like what you see?" Richard asked.

"It's fine. They now understand who owns who." Augustus looked across the square and watched as Lawrence approached them with a Nigger he didn't know. Augustus feared the regal man, for he had to be over seven feet tall, dressed in a royal garb. The stranger approached them as a supreme judge.

The men stopped before him. "Your time has come to an end Richard. You must leave here, at once. You have corrupted the holy."

Richard glared at Lawrence. "You called him? You're so impotent you called him?" Richard said. "Why did you call this Nigger? Are you trying to humiliate me?"

"Naw suh, I'se ain't. You'se did that at the Beginning before the Lawd and got put out 'fore it too," Lawrence told him with a smile.

"This isn't about Lawrence, Richard."

Richard found himself unable to speak. Albertus loosely knotted a thin, gold thread around him. Richard couldn't move.

The slaves gasped in disbelief. Who was this Negro who could bind a White man?

"Niggah—" Augustus said.

"Silence, little evil one," Albertus said.

Augustus turned red with fury, but he couldn't confute

him. Albertus considered the slaves witnessing the altercation. "Remember, there is a greater Master." Albertus considered his words, for he could only reveal so much to the witnesses. "Remember the words of the Supreme Master. Remember the words of your beloved Rabbi. Love one another. Love your neighbors as you would yourself." All standing about watched in awe as Albertus, a Negro, led away a White man, captive. The two disappeared once they rounded the bend.

"Ya'll git back to work," Augustus said.

"Massa, it's Sunday. You'se orderin' them to go to fields?" Lawrence said.

Augustus turned and left, followed by Lawrence.

New Orleans, Louisiana. Augustus 28, 1963

"Life on the plantation changed for the slaves after that day. Albertus' words had undone some of the damage done by Richard. However, the period of amnesty and good will didn't last long. Augustus wasted little time reinforcing the lesson he and Richard had worked for nearly a year to implement."

Julian sat before her, amazed. "Did it work?"

Lela nodded. "Yes. After about five years, once all those who had known Monsieur Emmanuel had passed away, the behaviors began to take a firm hold. Dare I say Augustus accelerated the demise of the old timers, many found dead under mysterious circumstances out by the Tangipahoa River. Once the old folks died, distrust and envy broke out like wildfire. After ten years, the younger generations had a latent distrust of one another they couldn't explain. It was the same on other plantations across the South.

"However, skin color preference was a little different on La Rose because of Sammie and Augustus' penchant for dark-skinned Negro women. So the lighter skinned women were envious of the darker skinned women. But with me, I was despised because I was white-skinned and favored because I was Augustus' daughter. So, all his dark-skinned children hated me, or so I believed. I learned once I left the plantation they didn't hate me as much as I had believed."

"It is all too much," Julian said in a whisper. "Maybe that's the reason why—"

"What Julian?"

"Why Blacks can't trust each other now. We're different from other ethnic groups. Our loyalty to one another is very weak. We will betray each other at the first opportunity."

Lela wiped away her tears. "You are correct. It's the very reason why."

Julian wished to cry for his people, but he suppressed his tears. "How can we change this about ourselves, Grandmère?"

Lela took her little one in her arms. Now he wished to eradicate the curse from the psyche of Negroes where he once couldn't wait to institute it. "God must fix it. And we must ask Him to do so. But we can't ask Him until we can see the curse for ourselves," Lela said with a whisper into his ear. Julian nodded. "We don't even know there is a curse upon us; however, once we recognize it, we can ask God to release us."

Chapter 5

Lela

My father married late in life. He only did so because he didn't want Amite society to believe him to be 'funny.' He couldn't take my mother as his wife, whom he'd been sleeping with since his youth. So, he decided to marry Emmie Sue Roberts in 1836.

Michael Roberts' plan had worked, but not as he may have believed. Augustus believed he could whip Michael at his own game. Besides, Michael had forked over a hefty dowry for Augustus to marry his little angel. Emmie Sue could fuck like a whore while presenting the façade of an upstanding belle of pedigree to St. Helena's social set. Augustus liked that about her.

Prior to the wedding, Augustus had received a letter from a man proclaiming to be his father, advising against the union. Augustus burned it.

La Rose Plantation. 1836

AUGUSTUS WAS IN love. Well, rather lust. He couldn't marry the one he desired, so what was the point? He wanted Sammie. She understood him, accepting all of him, both the holy and the profane.

Emmie Sue had never been a modest person. In fact, her reputation was so bad that no one would have her, even with her large dowry. All the boys in the parish had probably had her, anyway. Yet, Augustus couldn't pass up the gold, even if it came from his enemy.

Emmie Sue's family gave the couple a lavish wedding to commemorate the union. Every planter within a three-parish radius had traveled to La Rose Plantation to attend the social event of the season. As Augustus stood with Emmie Sue on the receiving line at the reception, he could barely maintain his decorum with his guests. These were the same people who gossiped about his family. Jealous motherfuckers.

Augustus heard the voice of a man he despised. He turned to find Josef Johannesen laughing with Michael Roberts and Emmie Sue's dim-witted mother, Emeline. Who had invited him? Probably Roberts, he determined. The two had always been good friends, more so snakes in a pit, as far as Augustus was concerned. Augustus had never forgiven Josef for sleeping with his girlfriend, Lucy, while they were in boarding school. She had claimed Josef had raped her.

Augustus doubted it. She was fucking him, so why would she cry rape after fucking Josef? He dumped her without delay and hadn't thought about her since. In any case, he never trusted Josef around his women again. He should've killed him then. He should have reviewed the guest list for the wedding.

Josef kissed Emmie Sue on the cheek, congratulating her.

"Keep your lips off my wife, you goddamn marsh Nigger."

Josef smiled. "Mrs. Chevalier. You are such a beautiful woman. I suspect you could've found someone better suited for you than this Frog," he said, suppressing the urge to shoot Augustus on his wedding day. "When you tire of him, you are always welcomed at Piney Woods Plantation."

"Is that so? Soon, you won't have a home," Augustus said. "Have you settled your debts with your buddies in New Orleans?"

Josef lunged for Augustus. Michael Roberts grabbed him. "Not today," Michael whispered in Josef's ear. "We'll deal with him later."

Josef freed himself from Michael's grasp and smoothed his jacket. "Come along," he said to his wife. He grabbed her hand and pulled her away. Emeline, standing beside her husband on the receiving line looked away, distressed by the altercation.

Josef's son, Hanzel, tarried behind, glaring at Augustus. "What are you going to do, you little cloggie?" Augustus said. "Run along, before I put your little ass in a pie and bake you." The child ran away.

"Augustus!" Emmie Sue said.

He pierced her soul, glaring into her eyes as if he would choke her on the spot. He put a smile on his face. "Bitch, if you ever contradict me again, I'll kill you. Do you hear me?" Augustus grabbed her hand as he whispered into her ear, feigning an intimate moment.

Ingesting the terror of her new husband's temper and promise of violence, she stood before him lifeless. Regaining control of her faculties, Emmie Sue turned to the next guest, masking her fear of her husband.

Augustus scanned the room to find Sammie standing along the wall in formal maid's attire. He made eye contact with her. Why had he forced her to do this? He knew why. He wanted her to believe she was just his slave and concubine. His face flushed and he looked away. Out of the corner of his eye, he saw Lawrence come in and lead Sammie away. Why would Lawrence take her now, once he had confessed in his heart he had wronged the one he loved?

The following day, the couple left Louisiana for a two-year honeymoon. They returned eight months later. Emmie Sue was four months pregnant.

After three days of labor, Emmie Sue bore Augustus a son. He named the boy Jean Charles Chevalier. He looked into the boy's sleeping face, feeling little passion and love for the child in his heart. Well, at least he had a boy to carry on his legacy. He hoped he would, anyway. The boy seemed soft to him. Well, Augustus figured, he was only a few minutes old. He could mold him and make him into a man. Augustus had hoped Emmie Sue would die in childbirth, but she'd survived.

Emmie Sue wasn't well after giving birth and couldn't nurse Jean Charles. Augustus forced Sammie to nurse his son, but she wouldn't give the child any milk. She made no effort to mask her anger towards Augustus. Her eyes made it plain she had no desire to nurse his wife's son.

For only the second time during the course of their relationship, Sammie had risen up against him. Augustus hadn't witnessed a level of rebellion and disdain in her since he'd sold off her sisters. Her behavior confused Augustus at first, but after a good tongue lashing, she conceded. He laughed. She would do as he commanded her. Sammie was his Nigger wife anyway, so what was the protest all about? It was her job to fuck him, cook his food, and attend to his children.

Augustus stood over her, watching as the baby pulled tirelessly on Sammie's dry tit. Sammie continued to glare at Augustus. Jean Charles began to whimper because he couldn't get any milk from her. The boy was too soft to cry for himself.

He snatched the child from Sammie's breast, taking him across the yard to one of his other women. She had just given birth to his child and had named the baby Nicka. She should've called her 'Nigga,' Augustus would joke to himself every time he thought of the child's name. He didn't want to be bothered with a child that dark. The child's dark complexion had proven to be good thing, for no one suspected the girl to be his. As soon as the child came of age, he would sell her off, as he had done with six others.

La Rose Plantation. 1839

After two years of marriage, Augustus had tired of his wife. He should never have married her, but he couldn't resist the wealth that came along with her hand. He didn't need the money, for he was wealthy in his own right. Nevertheless, he couldn't pass it up either. He had used the gold from her dowry as collateral for investments in a variety of different industries: whaling, alcohol distilleries, textiles, and a new industry called steel refining. Michael would have exploded if he had known of the hundreds of thousands of dollars he'd made off his marriage to Emmie Sue.

"Mis'sur?"

"What the fuck do you want, Lawrence?"

I could incinerate him, Most Holy Father, Lawrence prayed. He could hear his brothers and sisters in the presence of the Lord laughing. Let them try and deal with him. The Lord frowned at him. Lawrence surrendered to the will of the Lord, allowing Augustus to live. "Mis'sur and Ma'Dame Roberts are here. They're in the parlor with Ma'Dame Chevalier," Lawrence said. He turned and left.

"Goddammit!" Augustus didn't feel like being bothered with that asshole and his dumb ass wife. He poured himself a shot of bourbon, drank it, and left his library.

Augustus entered the parlor to find Emmie Sue with a baby on her knee. The child smiled at her, gurgling. "Who is this? Your bastard grandson?"

Michael refused to allow Augustus to ruin the moment. "Why no, Augustus. This is my son, James," Michael said.

Augustus stood beside his wife and looked at the child. The baby's happy demeanor faded. He had spooky eyes, as if he could look right through him. Augustus didn't care for the boy.

"Aren't you going to congratulate my parents, Augustus?"

"For what? The child looks nothing like your father. Perhaps I should congratulate your mother instead."

Michael dove for Augustus, knocking him to the floor. The men tussled about, beating each other without mercy. Struggling, each man retrieved their concealed firearms. Michael fired, but missed. Augustus sat atop him, placing the mussel of his pistol between Michael's eyes. Emeline screamed and ran from the room. "Too bad you won't live to see your wife's son grow up, Michael." Augustus' skin felt prickly.

Lawrence entered the room and stood over the two men. He snatched the pistol from Augustus' hand. Emmie Sue feared the sudden move would set the gun off, but it hadn't. Augustus stood up and left.

"WHO'SE THAT, LAWRENCE?" Sammie looked up from her work shelling peas as he entered the kitchen with the baby.

Lawrence dried his face. He couldn't stop crying. "This here is Prince James."

"Prince?"

"I'se mean James."

Sammie nodded as she studied Lawrence. He didn't even seem to care for Jean Charles as much as he did for this child. "Well, who'se baby is that?"

"He's Emmie Sue's brother," he said, oblivious to Sammie's shock and dismay.

Sammie smiled at the child and then went to tend the fire. She couldn't understand how a couple the Roberts' age could have a child. Once the fire was burning to her satisfaction, she stood and turned toward Lawrence and the child. They were gone.

After three hours of visiting, Michael had had enough. "Get the boy, Emeline. It's time to go."

Emeline smiled and lowered her head. She wished to stay longer, but she knew better than to challenge her husband. "I enjoyed you today, Emmie Sue," she said. She kissed her daughter. "Come and help me with your brother." The women left the parlor, headed for the nursery.

Arriving at the nursery, the women couldn't find James or his nurse. Jean Charles napped alone, in his crib. Emmie Sue raced into the hallway. "Papa!"

Michael ran from the parlor and stood in the center of the foyer, looking up to the second floor. "What is it darling?" Dread filled Michael's heart, seeing the look of concern on his daughter's face. He frowned, watching Augustus entering the foyer from his library.

"James is gone!"

Michael turned to Augustus. "What have you done with my son?"

"Nothing. Maybe the dog ran off with him," Augustus said, unconcerned. Michael charged him and then swung, but Augustus ducked his punch.

"Will you two stop fighting and help us find him?" Emmie Sue said.

The men squelched their hatred for each other and searched the home for the child.

The men searched the mansion, but they could find neither James nor his nurse. They went to the attic to search for him; perhaps one of the slaves had hidden the boy there. The heat and humidity of the third floor was suffocating. Lawrence was the only slave who lived on the floor. Lawrence's willingness to live there confirmed Augustus' suspicions he must be some sort of devil to be able to endure the stifling heat. All the other house slaves had chosen to live in the quarters rather than bear the oppressive conditions of the third floor.

Arriving at Lawrence's door, the men barged in. A cool breeze greeted them. There sat Lawrence with the child upon his lap wearing a little gold crown on his head. Lawrence bounced the baby on his knee, cooing and singing to him. James gurgled and laughed, batting his chubby little arms up and down.

Michael dove for Lawrence, but Augustus jumped him.

Augustus reserved for himself alone the delight of beating his property, unwilling to share the pleasure. He wouldn't even allow the overseer beat the slaves. All punishment on the plantation came from his hand.

The men separated themselves. Lawrence stared at the two, bewildered. "What ya'll doin'?"

Michael searched the room, unable to find the boy. Lawrence continued to stare at him, confused. "Where's my goddamn son?"

"I'se reckon he's in the nursery with Jean Charles, Mis'sur Roberts," Lawrence said.

Augustus and Michael left Lawrence's room and rushed downstairs to the nursery. They burst in the door, finding the children asleep in their cribs. James' nurse sat in her rocking chair, reading a book. Once she noticed the men, the nurse stood from the comfort of her chair and began to prepare James to leave.

"I'm taking my boy home and getting him away from all these voodoo hatching Niggah's you keep on this place," Michael said to Augustus.

"Fuck you too, Michael. And take your little bitch home with you."

Michael couldn't punch him, for he held his son. "Emmie Sue, I got him." Michael left the nursery. "Find your mother so we can leave."

Chapter 6

New Orleans, Louisiana. August 28, 1963

Julian had so many questions, but he knew better than to interrupt his grandmère.

"You may ask me, young man," Lela said.

Julian snickered. "Kinda inbred, huh Grandmère?"

Lela scowled, ready to pop him in his mouth. Nevertheless, the child had spoken the truth. How could she be angry with him? "Yes." She laughed a little. "It worked for the children of Adam and Eve, didn't it? The practice has served our family as well." Lela sighed, looking away. She wanted to make her child feel guilty, yet at the same time she found it all a bit entertaining and naughty. She concealed her amusement.

Julian felt a little bad. He feared he may have offended her. "I'm sorry."

"There is nothing to be sorry for. You're correct." She patted his knee. "Many years later, once the Lord had revealed these things to us, Nancy said, 'the blood is tight.'

And it is. But, it's that way for a reason."

Julian nodded, accepting Lela's reply. Another question popped up in his mind. "Why did Lawrence treat James like a prince?"

Lela didn't understand. "Because he is. I mean, he was."

"So what? Are you a princess of some sort?"

Lela gazed into his eyes, ravishing his soul. "No my darling, I'm not. I am the Queen."

La Fourche Parish. February, 1841

SARAH THE SLAVE stood at the swamp's edge bordering the Gulf of Mexico in La Fourche Parish. She walked through the vine ensnared land, out to the small peninsula that jutted out into the gulf, bowing to the west. The cool breeze, laced with warmness, comforted her. *I should go*, she told herself, but she knew she couldn't. Sarah had surrendered to his will. She watched as the sun set on the world.

She reclined upon the earth, unconcerned with the animals and insects which traversed about her. They wouldn't come near her. They knew her, as she knew them. They both respected one another. The beasts of the Earth would allow her to rest. Sarah looked up into the night sky and spotted a shooting star. Comforted, she smiled for a moment and drifted into her slumber. The alligators and cottonmouths stood guard about her.

Sarah opened her eyes to find the moon bathing her. She returned to her rest.

Aroused from her dreams, she found one standing before her clothed in the light of heaven. He reclined beside her. "You'se ain't mine. You can't do this thang," Sarah said in a whisper, terrified of what was to come.

"I will not, if you deny me," he said. He kissed her.

Sarah called his name. "This ain't right. Your blood is mine," she said.

"Only if you allow it, can it be. What I have for you is a great gift. No shame will come upon you or your house."

Sarah's face twisted in torment. She couldn't deny him. She could see his gift as well. She nodded in consent.

Taking her in his arms he loved her, he entered her with a force and authority she'd never known.

Sarah gasped.

Laboring to open her eyes, she found the face of her husband Teddy, her love. Yet it wasn't him and she knew it. Nevertheless, she couldn't turn away her lover. She received him and his gift.

The morning light awoke her, the alligators having returned to the waters which surrounded her. Sarah cried. "I'se sorry, Teddy. I'se couldn't resist him." Taking the hem of her skirt, she wiped away the wetness from between her legs.

Yet, there was no way she could wipe away the one who now dwelled within her. She dried her tears and returned home.

La Rose Plantation. Summer, 1841

"WHAT'S WRONG WITH yah?" Sarah seemed weak to Teddy and sluggish too. She hadn't left the plantation in weeks. She should have come and gone several times, helping escapees find their way to freedom.

She smiled at her husband, wishing to conceal her guilt. "We'se gonna have a son."

"What?" Teddy sat on the side of the bed, filled with disbelief. Another child? He cherished his little Missy, but a son? Teddy had dreamed of the unborn child, tall and strong, just like him, but he had never shared the visions with Sarah. "When do you'se think he'll be born?"

Sarah wiped away her tears of joy and sorrow. "Late, after the harvest."

Sarah lay on the little straw-stuffed bed in their cabin, soaked with perspiration. It had been a difficult delivery. Missy's birth had been effortless compared to this one.

Teddy held his wife in his arms. Sammie bathed the child, washing away the fluids of her nephew's former home. She passed the boy to Teddy, placing the child in his arms.

With much effort, Sarah opened her eyes and turned her

head toward her son and her husband. "Whatcha gonna call him, Teddy?"

Teddy smiled at the boy and kissed his forehead, tasting his wife on the child's brow. "Toot. I'se means Toussaint."

"Toussaint?"

"Yessum. He's holy to me," Teddy said, full of emotion. He didn't understand why he had chosen the name. He hadn't ever heard the name before. Oh yes, he had. Some of the slaves had whispered of a deliverer named Toussaint, who had led a slave rebellion somewhere far away. He had always hoped to have a son who would deliver the slaves in Louisiana to their freedom.

Teddy cried. The little one in his arms seemed to giggle and then return to his dreams. Teddy laid the child on his mother's breast so he could nurse. Teddy kissed her, and then left their cabin to announce his son's birth to the slave community.

Sarah guided her breast into Toussaint's mouth. Instinct compelled him to accept it, draining the little strength which remained in her body.

In her delirium, Sarah saw her lover standing before her. "Our son is beautiful."

"Yessah, devil," Sarah said.

"You know that not to be the case."

Sarah said nothing.

Her lover placed a rose and a key upon the child. "Keep this key. He will need it once he's a man."

Too weak to pick it up, Sarah watched as the key levitated above both her and her nursing child. It floated across the room. A little box appeared on the rickety wooden table. The key came to rest inside of it. The lid snapped closed and the box disappeared from sight.

Sarah slept with her son at her breast.

Chapter 7

La Rose Plantation. 1842

Augustus hated the kiss asses who sat around his table. He finished his Bourbon. His guests had attended the dinner party because they feared him and desired a free meal. He relished their fear. How had Emmie Sue convinced him to host a party for all the planters in the parish? He remembered her argument. Filthy little whore. She understood how to get what she wanted from him.

Michael Roberts walked in with his wife and their son. Michael was a bastard if Augustus had ever met one. Augustus had figured out long ago that Michael loved no one but Emmie Sue, his pride and joy, probably because she was just like him: a liar, a thief, and a manipulator. Everyone in the parish knew Michael treated his wife like trash, but not Emmie Sue. It delighted Augustus to abuse Michael's little pearl. Every punch he landed on her was a blow he landed on his enemy.

Augustus figured Michael believed him to be a fool. He knew Michael hoped to kill him while still married to his daughter, the whore. Then he could claim the Chevalier fortune and lands for himself. Augustus laughed within, for he knew Emmie Sue would have the earth tossed atop her long before he ever would. Augustus had already won, for he had accepted no less than ten thousand dollars in gold for her hand. The only reason Michael paid it was because he expected to get it back, with interest.

Augustus stared at the child in Michael's arms. Why would he carry a boy his age? He should make his little ass walk. He could never remember the child's name; he didn't care to know it anyway. The Roberts boy was strange to Augustus, but he couldn't quite figure out why. He hated looking into the child's eyes. He had one of those 'seeing souls,' as Lawrence would say. Michael placed the child on the floor and Sammie led him away to the children's table, to eat with Jean Charles and the others.

Once everyone had been seated, Emmie Sue stood before her guests in a green silk dress Augustus had never seen before. He liked it. It pushed up her little tits, making her appear more desirable.

"I would like to thank all of you for honoring Augustus and me with your presence this evening," Emmie Sue said, sweeter than shit. "I'm delighted to present to you my cousin, Marion Clemens," she said, placing her hand on his shoulder. "He has just returned to Louisiana from school. I'm proud to say my Marion has graduated from the Medical Institution at Yale College in Connecticut!"

The dinner guests cheered and applauded, nodding their heads with pride for their hometown son. "So if any of ya'll have any troubles, doncha hesitate to call on my Maury," Emmie Sue said in response to the warm laughter of her guests. She bent over and kissed Marion on the cheek, with much affection.

Sammie wheeled the serving platter into the dining room and handed the carving knife to Augustus.

So, this is Maury. Augustus had heard she had a cousin named Maury whom she was particularly fond of. She was bit too fond of him, as rumor dictated. That must have been her reason for introducing him as Marion a few days before.

Lawrence removed the baroque silver lid of the serving platter, revealing the beautiful, young roasted pig with an apple in its mouth, garnished with grapes and oranges.

His eyes fell on his wife at the opposite end of the table, entranced with every word Marion uttered.

Augustus made the first cut.

Chapter 8

La Rose Plantation. 1843

Emmie Sue stopped having sex with Augustus once Marion came to town. He knew a slut like his wife couldn't go over a year without getting it. Not that Augustus cared, for he had Sammie. Sex was different with Sammie. He could now admit to himself he loved her. But she would turn on him if she got the chance. However, deep in his heart, he knew that she wouldn't. Dumb Nigger.

Augustus decided to sleep in the house instead of at Sammie's. Sammie didn't like for him to stay there because she feared the other slaves would shun her. He had asked her once if anyone had and she'd told him no. He watched as a little smile crept across her face. She was telling the truth. In any case, Sarah had already told him life had changed for her in the slave community.

He wondered if anyone had ever told her about what had happened that day, down by the river. He knew no one had. Just as well. Augustus extinguished the lamp and crawled into bed, exhausted. He'd experienced few troubles with the slaves after that day. Sammie seemed happier, the slave women embracing her and inviting her to their little slave functions.

Only Sarah gave him grief about the execution, but not really. She hated the women who had mistreated her sister. Sneaky Nigger. Augustus knew she only wanted him to do her dirty work. He snuggled into his pillow. He had been more than happy to oblige.

He heard the door to his room open, awaking him from his twilight slumber. He pulled his pistol from between the mattress and the bed frame. Emmie Sue. What was she doing in his room, uninvited? What if Sammie had been with him? He started to tell her to get out, but when she took him in her mouth, he got over it. She fucked him harder than she had when they had conceived Jean Charles.

ALTHOUGH HE HATED her, he couldn't stand to see her suffer. She had been in bed for a month. They couldn't figure out what was wrong with her.

The opening door diverted his attention from his newspaper. Sarah brought in a bottle of bourbon. He had sent Sammie to the cellar to fetch it. Why would she send her sister to deliver it? His skin became prickly, realizing Sammie probably hadn't. "What are you doin' in the house, Sarah?

Stay out in the yard with the rest of the Niggers."

Sarah didn't reply. She uncorked the bottle, and then turned to leave. "Emmie Sue's been sick," Augustus said against his will.

Sarah stood at the door with her back to him. "Why'se you reckon she don't get better?"

"I don't know."

"Maybe you'se should ask her doctor," Sarah said as she left, closing the door.

Augustus went to pour himself a drink. The glass shattered in his hand, raining bourbon all over his pants.

Emmie Sue's condition didn't improve. She couldn't keep any food down and accused Sammie of trying to poison her. She had even mustered the energy to take her soup to the kitchen and hurl it at Sammie. The bowl hit her on the head, knocking her unconscious.

When Augustus returned home that evening, Lawrence told him what had happened. He ran up the stairs, ready to kill her, but Lawrence stopped him. Augustus ordered the slaves to hitch the carriage. He sent Emmie Sue home to her father. He was tired of her sick ass anyway.

Michael brought Emmie Sue back to La Rose three days later, with her cousin, the doctor, in tow. Michael explained to Augustus her condition hadn't improved and his wished for the doctor to examine her.

"Why not allow him examine her at your place?"

"This is her home Augustus," Michael said, frustrated. "Even you can see how ill she is. Shouldn't she rest and recuperate in her own bed?"

Augustus considered her as one of the slaves carried her upstairs. She had lost weight and looked pitiful. Augustus felt a little guilty. "Alright," he said, following them upstairs.

IN THE DAYS since her return, Augustus had begun to feel affection for his wife. She seemed so helpless, depending on him for everything. She had told Augustus she was dying, and he believed her.

Dr. Clemens stood before the couple, ready to give them his prognosis. He seemed nervous to Augustus, making him anxious as well. Although he'd wished Emmie Sue dead for years, he had reconsidered, now that the moment had arrived. He wanted her around. After all, she did serve a purpose in his life, socially at least. He couldn't take Sammie anywhere.

Augustus held Emmie Sue in his arms, protecting her from the doctor's words. They watched as Marion wiped his brow. Augustus grew impatient. "What's wrong with her?"

Startled at first by Augustus' outburst, Dr. Clemens relaxed and then smiled with joy. "You're going to be a father, Monsieur Augustus. Congratulations!" Marion extended his hand.

Augustus allowed his hand to hang in mid-air. He looked from Emmie Sue to Dr. Clemens. He remembered the night she came in to him. "How far along is she?"

Dr. Clemens became a bit agitated, as if doing the math in his head. "Three months."

It had been two months since he was last with Emmie Sue, after a year apart.

Liars

"The good wishes are all yours, Dr. Clemens," Augustus said. The color drained from Emmie Sue's face. She began to cry. Augustus left her side on the bed. "You should comfort your whore, the mother of your child, Dr. Clemens," Augustus said. "I'm going to kill you for getting my wife pregnant, that I promise you. I always keep my promises to those I hate. If I see you in this house again, I'll kill you sooner than I'd intended."

Augustus left. He could hear Emmie Sue crying for him, but he continued his trek to his library. He grabbed the decanter of bourbon from the buffet and drank from it.

Women are whores. Irresistible little whores. His mother had been one. Now his wife. He loved his mother, but not his wife. He went to see Sammie. He barged into her little house without announcement.

Sammie sat up in bed, finding Augustus standing before her with the moon light illuminating his face. She could see the hurt in his eyes. He'd found out about Ma'Dame and the doctor. Everyone on the plantation had known of the affair, catching them in the fields, in cabins, everywhere. Even slaves from neighboring plantations shared gossip about the two with the La Rose slaves, which they had overheard from their masters.

At first, she believed Augustus would be mad at her for not telling him. But instead, a hurt little red-faced boy stood in her doorway, too devastated to be concerned with her keeping the secret from him. She opened her arms and he fell into them. Hot angry tears rolled down his face, but he refused to cry out. Sammie stroked his hair, soothing him. He found comfort in her embrace and fell asleep in her arms.

Six months later, Emmie Sue gave birth to her daughter. Augustus refused to look at the child. "What should we call her, Augustus?" Emmie Sue lay in bed, exhausted from the travails of birth.

"I don't name bastards that ain't mine, Emmie Sue." She had soiled his bed with the birth of her daughter. Why couldn't she have the baby in her own bed? But then again, it had already been soiled when she accepted the seed of another man upon it. *Slut.* "Why not ask the good doctor what to name her? But then again, he's only a little more than a child himself. Is he even twenty-one years old?"

Emmie Sue couldn't muster the energy to have the same fight with him which she'd endured for the last six months. "She's yours, Augustus."

He left them. Augustus went to the stable, mounted Rock and rode hard to New Orleans. He retired into the arms of his favorite whore, Madame Tessy, and forgot his troubles at home. He didn't think of home for three months. The moment he returned, he kicked Emmie Sue and her newborn daughter out of his house, for good.

LAWRENCE TROTTED TO the front door. Someone pounded on it like a madman. His heart skipped a beat, worried that tragedy had befallen one of the slaves. He opened the door. Michael Roberts pushed past him, blazing a path to Augustus' library. Lawrence knew there would be trouble.

Michael burst in the door, only to meet the muzzle of Augustus' shotgun. "What the fuck is wrong with you, Roberts?"

"You think that you can turn my daughter out in the road like a whore?" Michael said.

"That's what she is, isn't she?"

Michael charged toward him, his revolver drawn. Augustus pumped his shot gun.

Lawrence stood in the background, waiting to see what would happen. Perhaps the men would kill each other and he could live in peace. Maybe he would leave La Rose for good and return to France and visit his brothers at the Roberts Château. He hadn't seen Jeffrey or Louis for at least one hundred years.

Or, maybe he would visit his brother Albertus in Ethiopia. He hadn't visited the Throne of the Most High for some time. He missed his brothers Mike, Gab, well everyone. They would always have such fun, traveling the universe together. He couldn't decide on how to enjoy his new found freedom.

Lawrence sighed, watching as Roberts back down. Coward. The men wouldn't annihilate each other as he had fantasized. Lawrence knew then he would never escape La Rose as long as it stood on the Earth.

"You're gonna make an honorable woman of my Emmie Sue and my Lily, Chevalier," Michael said. "You're going to take them back into this house!"

Augustus laughed. "Even the blood of Christ couldn't wipe the filth off that whore," he said, toying with the trigger of his shot gun. He lowered it, resigned not to kill his cousin. "She can stay with you. I ain't raising her cousin's baby. You do it. I'm divorcing her."

Michael panicked, knowing Augustus would love nothing better than to dump his daughter and keep her dowry, free and clear. "Without admitting any guilt whatsoever, for anyone can look at the child and tell she's yours; I'll give you one hundred acres of my land. Say it's a gift, commemorating little Lily's birth."

"Who's Lily?"

"Your daughter, asshole!"

Augustus considered his offer. Roberts owned some land adjacent to his. He had wanted it for years; however, he knew Michael would never sell it. "I want your land near Montpelier."

Michael wished to kill him and he would in time. "Fine. I'll have my lawyer draw up the papers." Michael stormed from the mansion, planning his revenge.

Chapter 9

La Rose Plantation. 1845

The slaves watched as the 'Sheddahs,' the name they'd given to the outcast slaves who worked in the 'Shed,' drag Timmy away. His wife jumped on one of the Sheddah's back. He tossed her off, and then kicked her without mercy. Timmy begged them to stop, explaining she was pregnant. They abandoned their torment of her and refocused their attention on Timmy. One of the men put a collar on his neck and dragged him away. His wife lay in the front yard before their cabin, bleeding. The other women picked her up and carried her inside the little cabin to attend to her. She miscarried before the sun rose.

ROCK SNORTED. THE beast fanned his tail about, creating a momentary breeze for Augustus. The slaves had failed to make their quota the week before, leaving the southern quadrant of cotton unattended. They could lose the crop. "I need a new overseer," Augustus said to himself as he crossed the little bridge over a small creek, leading to the southern lands. As soon as Rock crossed the bridge, he bucked Augustus without warning. The horse fled, terrified of the woman who blocked his path.

Augustus landed on his back, winded. He saw a gray slave dress and some locked hair fleeing a kerchief, or so he assumed. The sunlight stood to her rear, creating a silhouette of the woman standing before him as his judge. Medusa. He couldn't see the woman's face, but he knew exactly who had attacked him without ever raising her hand.

Augustus' breath returned to his lungs as the dust from the road settled upon him. He inhaled some it, causing him to cough violently. He spat out the dust laden mucus.

She approached him. Her shadow shaded him, dominating him.

"What the fuck?"

"You'se wrong, Augustus," Sarah the Slave said, snarling at him.

"When did you get back from the swamp, Niggah?" Augustus stood and dusted himself off. "You're gonna settle your sins with me before you're done, Sarah."

"I'se only hafta settle with God. You ain't him."

Augustus grabbed for her throat, but she disappeared. A power he couldn't see slammed him down on the dusty path, rendering him immobile.

Sarah stood over him and sneered. "You'se gonna pay for the blood you done split, 'Massa,'" she said. "You'se wrong about Timmy and you'se gonna pay for what you did to him." Sarah released him from her invisible grip.

Augustus scrambled up from the dirt. He searched for Sarah, but couldn't find her. "I ain't done nothing to that Niggah yet, but I'm going to. There's nothing you can do to stop me either." He felt something stick him in the back of the neck, as if a bee had stung him. He turned around to find Sarah standing behind him.

"You don't know what he did," Augustus said. "He helped one of my prize Niggah's escape! I paid seven hundred dollars for that buck. I could have studded him for years, and Timmy helps him run away. He's a dead Niggah!" A vein jutted forth on his forehead.

Sarah peered deep into his eyes. "You'se wrong, Augustus. Yo' neighbor stole Simmus and sold him from under you. If you'se keep Timmy in that shed, you'se gonna pay." Sarah looked out into the Spirit. Her face fell slack. "And if's you'se decides one day to spill my blood, you'se gonna die."

Sarah quelled her emotions, releasing the vision. She swirled her toe in the dust. "Yup. Your family gonna crumble if's you'se do it."

"You're gonna die you voodoo preaching bitch!" Augustus charged her.

She stood before him motionless, overcome with the vision of her future. Augustus threw his punch, aiming for her face. The forward motion of the attempted strike propelled him into a thorn studded bramble bush. He growled from the pain of the thorns' sting. After a few moments, he freed himself from the bush's embrace.

Sarah reappeared and stared at the red, bloodied and scarred man who stood before her. Disappointed, she turned and disappeared into the crops.

THE HINGES OF the wood plank door groaned as he opened it, choked with rust. He had considered having one of the slaves oil it, but he thought better of it. It provided a sort of ambience for what lay within.

When he first took over as master of La Rose, Augustus sent for items from the Chevalier Château in Fargniers, France, to furnish his special playhouse. He had visited the château during the summer of his seventeenth year, exploring not only the treasures on the estate, but also those which lay hidden in Paris' seedier districts.

While preparing to leave the château for an evening of fun, he leaned against staircase wall to fasten his shoe. Once he removed his weight from the wall, a concealed door popped open, revealing a flight of stairs leading downward.

He descended them to investigate, inhaling the musk and

dampness of the space. A spirit descended upon him, one of fear and suffering. His heart pounded hard in his chest.

Reaching the bottom, he stood before two ancient, heavy oak doors. The doors seemed to be twenty-four feet tall. He pulled on the round iron handle of the left door. Much to his surprise, it was unlocked. Using all of his strength, he opened it.

What he found inside amazed him. A torture chamber! He walked around the large room, admiring its different implements, its centerpiece a stone fire pit. He appraised the chains with cuffs mounted at their ends, embedded in the stone walls and floors. Hooks hung suspended by long iron chains from the ceiling.

He couldn't believe the many different types tools displayed on the stoned walls of the chamber: hammers, daggers, swords, and chains with spiked iron balls attached to their ends. Flails. He particularly liked those.

Immobilized, he halted his tour of the chamber before the iron maiden. She took his breath away. She was beautiful. She gazed into his eyes, enticing him with her twisted smile to enter. He had read about them in school. "Once I'm master, I will bring you to La Rose," he said in a whisper to the smiling lady, caressing her side with his fingertips.

"No, you won't, young man."

Augustus jumped so high he thought he would impale

himself into the stone ceiling. "Papa, what are you doing here?"

"You didn't know I was here?"

"No."

Emmanuel placed his arm around his son's shoulder. The boy was now taller than him. "You're correct. You will one day become master of La Rose. You may take whatever you wish from here." Emmanuel frowned. "However, you cannot take Mademoiselle. She is wed to me alone, mon fils." Wickedness cascaded across Emmanuel's face, sparking fear in Augustus' heart. "Oui, mon fils. She is my lady. I created her for this room, alone."

Augustus smiled, recalling his cherished days with his father in France that summer. He hadn't enjoyed such a good time with his father since his childhood, when they'd visited New Orleans. His mood soured, remembering how he himself had ruined the trip by telling his father of his mother's affair. Augustus pushed the thought from his mind. He refocused his mounting fury on the traitor awaiting him down below. Augustus descended the stone stairs.

He enjoyed torturing Timmy, his screams soothing his wrath. Chained spread eagle between the ceiling and the floor, Augustus found the task of skinning him alive simple.

He'd experienced more trouble gutting hogs during slaughter time. Once he completed his task, Timmy died quickly. Five hundred dollars wasted, but so what? "Don't steal from me," Augustus said to Timmy's skinless corpse. He spat on the body, the liquid oozing down his exposed facial muscles. "Burn him," he said to the Sheddahs as he left.

AUGUSTUS VISITED HIS slave trader, Jans. He always gave him a good deal on runaways. Usually, these slaves tended to be top quality males with a rebellious spirit. They proved hard for Jans to move, for they were repeat offenders and hard to break. Augustus brought them at seventy percent below market value. After the runaways endured three days of plantation 'orientation' in the Shed, they broke. He enjoyed breaking them. He had yet to encounter a runaway Nigger he couldn't convert into a lap dog-.

Jans ordered his men to chain and collar the five new slaves Augustus had agreed to purchase. They exchanged money and Jan gave him the deeds for his acquisitions. "Yeah, I just sold one of your Niggah's."

Augustus placed the deeds inside of his leather wallet. "You ain't sold none of my Niggers."

Jans removed his hat and ran his fingers through his greasy, nit-riddled hair. "Naw, I'm certain of it. Michael Roberts sold him. He said he'd won him from you in a poker game." He put his hat back on his head.

Augustus listened as Jans rattled off his story of how Roberts had presented a deed to him, recording Augustus' sale of Simmus to him. Jans went on to tell him he had sold the slave for one thousand dollars.

Jans laughed at Augustus. "A Nigger like that? Hell, you couldda studded that Nigger for the next thirty years, easy. He's only 'bout 18 years old. And you lost him to Roberts for five hundred?" Jans could hardly contain his amusement. "Got any more you wanna gamble away?"

Augustus resisted the urge to kill him in front of the slave auction house. Sensing a presence behind him, Augustus turned to see Sarah pass on the road. She looked at him and continued on her way. Augustus ran out into the road to grab her, but she had disappeared.

Three months had passed since he had killed Timmy.

LAWRENCE KICKED THE front door. Soon, his alarm was answered by Sallie. Lawrence carried Emmie Sue indoors with her holding little Lily in her arms. "Oh Lawd!" Sallie took the child from Emmie Sue.

Standing at the door of his parlor, Michael watched the surreal scene unfold. He couldn't figure out why she wore a veil and was dressed all in black. Lawrence headed for the stairs.

"Wait, Lawrence," Emmie Sue said.

Her speech sounded labored and slurred to Michael, as if her tongue was swollen. She handed a note to her father. "I'm ready, Lawrence," Emmie Sue said. Lawrence began his journey upstairs.

"Why are you veiled, Emmie Sue?" She didn't answer him. "Lawrence, stop!" Michael approached her, fearing what he would find beneath the heavy veil. Mustering his resolve, he lifted it, finding her face misshapen and swollen. Deep blues and purples coursed down her neck, disappearing beneath the neckline of the dress. Michael turned red, enraged Augustus would beat his daughter. He wondered if he had taken her to his rumored torture chamber. Michael could hear Emeline and Sallie screaming in the background of his nightmare. However, silence ranged in his ears. "Take her upstairs."

Michael wailed once he heard her bedroom door close. After a time, he regained control of his emotions. His granddaughter stared at him in confusion. Was the child accustomed to seeing her mother battered and bruised? "Sallie, take Lily and put her in the nursery with James." He felt the heat of rage flush through him. "And fetch the doctor."

Sallie nodded. "Should I'se send for the sheriff too, Mis'sur?"

"Did I ask you to, Nigger? Just do as I told you," he said,

not in the mood for her problem solving. Sallie took Lily upstairs. "Go and look after Emmie Sue," he said to his wife. Emeline scurried up the stairs, slamming the door shut once she entered her daughter's room.

Michael collapsed and wept at the bottom of the stairs, destroyed. Once the wave of grief passed, he opened the letter.

A daughter for a Nigger

Michael balled up the note and threw it on the floor. He would kill Augustus if it was the last thing he did.

Chapter 10

La Rose Plantation. 1846

It had been some time since they had attended Sunday Meeting as a family. In recent months, Sarah had been away from home so much, she never had time for her family. She'd spent much of her time with Araminta Ross, encouraging her and raising within her the strength of heart to champion her people and lead them out of bondage. However, her time had yet to come. Sarah smiled as she peered into the future, seeing that Araminta would change her name, as prophets tended to do once their time had come to serve the Lord. Harriet Tubman. "Good name, Araminta. You'se gonna serve Our Lawd well wit' that name," Sarah said to Araminta's soul.

Sarah continued to assist runaway slaves wishing to escape their lives of bondage, smoothing out their respective paths to freedom. She had spirited away many runaways, saving them from imminent capture and even death, in some cases. She laughed to herself, remembering many instances when the slave catchers had their prey in their grasp, pinned against a fence, or maybe a tree. Sarah would appear within their midst, telling the runaways to take each other's hand. She would then take the hand of the ones on either side of her and form a human chain. Within a fraction of a second, they all found themselves transported to Canada, or where ever the Lord chose to set them down. *God is good*, Sarah said to herself.

However, she had decided to spend this particular Sunday morning with her Teddy and her little son, Toot. She didn't see anyone running away from their captivity in the Spirit, so why not take the opportunity to spend time with her family? Sitting in her favorite chair on the porch, she watched her husband and her son walk away with their fishing poles planted on their shoulders like rifles, as if soldiers in the army. Toussaint was the spitting image of Teddy! Sarah's eyes misted.

"My, he looks every bit like your husband and nothing like his father."

She spat, propelling the fluid off the side of the porch into the grass. "Teddy is his father," Sarah fished her corn cob pipe out of her apron pocket and stuck in her mouth, in defiance. Barachiel struck a match off the bottom of his shoe and attempted to light her pipe, but she pushed away his hand, causing him to burn himself.

He sat and leaned back in the chair, rolled a cigarette, and lit it. "Now, is that any way to treat the father of your only son?"

Sarah scowled. "What do you want?"

"I only wish to admire our son. He is magnificent! He will do great things upon the Earth. He is the Protector of the Lord's Rose. He will walk the Earth after the End of Times. He will raise up the Lord's Baton." Barachiel stood from his chair and danced a quick jig. "Yes, he will hold the hand of the Most High God's Baton. Some may even fancy him as the Twin of the Savior."

He invited Sarah to join him in praise and revelry, but instead, she rolled her eyes at him and folded her arms beneath her breast. Barachiel continued his testimony. "He will stand until the End of Times. He will not die, although Satan will do his best to kill him."

Sarah could see his words were true, but refused to encourage him. She still hadn't forgiven him, or herself. "I shouldda gone to work today," Sarah said, kicking a pebble off the porch. She looked out in the Spirit once more, but saw nothing. Sure, there were a few folks out there plotting their escape from slavery's bondage, but no one on the run. Who would run in broad daylight anyway? She sighed. She was stuck with him.

"I'm afraid so, *ma fille.*"

Sarah's face turned to stone. "You'se a sick— Doncha call me that ever again. You'se here me? NEVER!"

Barachiel's jovial nature fell away. He had forgotten how modern man ransomed by Christ's blood found such activities disgusting. The Daughters of Eve had considered little of the practice. Although the practice wasn't encouraged, it wasn't considered as appalling either, back then.

Barachiel shuddered at the collective repulsion of Man reading Genesis 19 regarding Lot and his daughters. *That was different,* he debated with Heaven. Yet, he knew the transgression was the same. "I'm sorry, Sarah."

Sarah watched as her son and her husband turned the corner. She pursed her lips. "I'm not. I'se ain't happy 'bout how he got here, but I'se can't imagine my life without my joy. I'se would never deny my boy and I'se cain't never regrets him bein' here. If the Good Lawd didn't want him here, he wouldn't be. God blessed me wit' that boy, so who is I to complain about how the Lawd sent him?"

Barachiel patted her shoulder, focusing on the future. "Do you see her? Soon, our Rose will be with us."

She smiled with joy. "Yessah. I'se sees her," Sarah said. Barachiel and Sarah the Slave watched as Sammie crossed the path between the cabins. Once she reached the other side, she stopped and rubbed the small of her back. "She don't knows it yet," Sarah said. "I'se gonna go wit' her," Sarah said to Barachiel, but she found herself alone. She ran from the porch and joined her sister, walking hand and hand to the pond.

"What's wrong with you?"

Sammie grimaced as he mounted her. She couldn't believe he'd even noticed she wasn't well. Then again, she wasn't surprised by his insensitivity to her discomfort. "I'se dunno."

Liar. "Yeah, you do. You go to see your voodoo ass sister?" Augustus entered her. She was different, her vagina sucking the life out of him. He feared he would yell out.

"Yessah. I'se did, Gus."

He loved it when she called him Gus. His orgasm mind-bending, he yelled loud enough for everyone in the slave quarters to hear. Hell, like they didn't know anyway. They surely would turn a deaf ear to whatever they heard coming from Sammie's house, after being presented with the fate of gossipers many years before. "Well, what did that evil ass bitch have to say?" He rolled off her, his nerves still twitching from the orgasm that wouldn't end.

Sammie curtailed her emotions. "I'se wit' child."

Before he could stop himself, a smile broke across his face. "You are?"

Sammie felt a little reassured, but afraid at the same time.

Augustus was notorious for selling off his Negro children. "Yeah, Gus. Sarah says she's a girl. She looks just like yah," she said through her tears.

He wondered how Sarah could know, but then he remembered that Sarah was some sort of witch. He kissed Sammie. It must be true if Sarah had said it; although he wanted to kill her evil ass. "It must be so," he said.

Sammie couldn't remember Augustus being as loving and tender with her since the death of his mother, Camille.

New Orleans, Louisiana. August 28, 1963

LELA OPENED HER eyes as Julian continued to rock the swing, transporting her back into the realm of 'what is.' She feared him to be asleep at first, but soon found he wasn't. She laughed, remembering him as a five-year-old, before Robert and Josephine took him to Europe once they married. He was a disagreeable child, but loving at the same time. The child had possessed an ornery spirit. She would laugh at him in those days. Robert only seemed to provoke him. Josephine spoiled him. But it was Lela who soothed him, convincing him to receive and to submit to reason.

Lela looked up into the sky, considering the construction and design of the wispy clouds. She closed her eyes once again, for a moment, and then reopened them. The clouds had ordered themselves into an ornate frame, displaying a window within their borders. Locked upon its center, Lela gazed within, becoming lost to the physical world. Her spirit sailed through the cloud-window into another world, presented for her perusal.

Lela. La Rose Plantation. February 12, 1847

MAMAN SMILED DOWN at me, full of pride and love, as if she had taken the love of God and created the sun and moon of her own volition. She embraced her masterpiece within her arms. I didn't know she smiled down on me back then, blessing me as holy and good, but I can see it now. I couldn't see her broad grin, for I was only a few hours old with my eyes yet to open; nevertheless, I remember her love now.

I can still feel her warmth, her energy. She felt as a volcano poised to erupt, the intense heat of her lava churning just below the surface. Yet, her explosion never came to pass. Her heat enveloped me, protecting me from all danger. Through her, I received comfort and strength, for I couldn't have ingested this supreme love from her milk alone.

I was loved.

She kissed me. "You'se mine," Maman said to me just above a whisper, knowing it not to be true. Although I was her flesh, I didn't belong to her. Another owned both Maman and me.

A barrier came between us and the candlelight. She looked up. "Dis her."

He scooped me from her arms. I can now hear his thoughts. He considered me, finding me so delicate, just like him in every way. Well, not every way. I was a Nigger. But who would know, he reasoned. He worried I may change, darkening up like the others, but he didn't believe so. He believed me to be different. My spirit could hear him whisper in his soul that Jean Charles didn't compare to me. His daughter Lily didn't even rank. He'd declared her to be a bastard.

He rocked me a bit in his arms, his affection for me growing. He frowned, mustering up within his soul indifference and hatred for me. He resisted the urge to kiss me. My eyes fluttered. I smiled, and then surrendered to my slumber. I only wished to greet and love him in my innocence. I slept. He loved me, but then he didn't. He returned me to my mother's arms.

"Call her Lela."

Augustus left the cook house, leaving his love and me, his sin, behind.

La Rose Plantation. February 20, 1847

SAMMIE STOOPED AT the hearth to light a small fire, adjacent to the main cooking fire. She winced in pain, still sore from Lela's birth. She smiled thinking of her daughter, thanking God for blessing her. Over the years of sleeping with Augustus, she had come to believe she couldn't have children.

Hanging a small pot above the fire she had just started, she poured some water into it and then added some rice. She added a bit of salt. Feeling someone behind her, she jumped up. The sudden movement caused her to spur a discharge, for she was still healing from Lela's birth. Yet, she soon forgot it, as her adrenalin surged. The basket where Lela had slept was gone. She panted, trying not to hyperventilate. "It's aw'rite," she said to calm herself. She ran from the kitchen, down the hall to Augustus' library.

Sammie threw open the door without knocking. Augustus looked up from his newspaper. "You'se gots her?"

The hairs stood up on his neck. "Who?"

"Lela! Where's my baby?"

Augustus leapt from his chair and took Sammie in his arms. He patted her back and led her from the room.

AUGUSTUS AND SAMMIE, along with the other house slaves, searched every room, but they couldn't find the baby. He called for Lawrence, but he'd failed to appear. Augustus wondered if Emmie Sue or Michael had taken the child. They could've easily slipped in, especially with Lawrence missing. But they didn't know Lela was his child. He'd managed to hide it from Emmie Sue, for she'd spent the better part of Sammie's pregnancy at her father's home. He had only allowed her to return to La Rose once Lela had been born.

He could hear Sammie wailing somewhere within the mansion as she searched for her child. The smell of sage burning filled his nostrils. Suddenly, Augustus had an ideal. "Sammie!"

She looked up to the second floor, watching as Augustus ran up to the third floor. She raced up the stairs.

Reaching the third floor landing, Sammie stopped. She saw Augustus standing in the doorway of Lawrence's room, paralyzed. As if time had ended, it took a lifetime for her to reach his side. She stood beside him, unable to believe the sight.

"You both may enter."

Augustus and Sammie entered the room. No longer a little room in the attic, the couple looked around the cathedral inside, constructed of white marble. Was it heaven? The space was enormous, seemingly capable of accommodating thousands of worshippers. Sammie's eyes turned to the altar, constructed of gold. Red roses covered it. Within its center was her infant daughter, lying in her humble wicker basket. A gold crown sat upon her head, embedded with rubies. She slept within, wearing her little burlap shift Sammie had made for her.

Augustus stood before the assembly in disbelief, observing the worshippers. They sang praises to God. They sang, "La Rose, La Rose, praise God Most High for the gift of his Rose on Earth!" The men and women were all of different races. Many were of tremendous size and height. Giants. Some appeared overjoyed by the presentation of the child, while others scowled, unable to contain their disdain and hatred for little Lela.

The congregation bowed to the altar. Augustus found himself on his knees, with Sammie bowing with him in tandem. He feared God. Augustus inhaled hard. At either end of the altar, two men stood. One was his Uncle Richard, who stood to the right, and his father Emmanuel stood at the left. Emmanuel smiled, and then as he turned and bowed to the one upon the altar. Richard scowled, and then turned to the altar. He fell to his knees, as if forced to do so by an unseen hand.

Augustus turned, feeling a presence. A dark-skinned man, dark like tar, approached the altar from the rear of the Cathedral. He wore the whitest robes with a train that seemed to go on for eternity. His robes continued to billow and flow, growing in length, as he approached the altar. He stood before the child and prayed.

"Beloved, we stand before God Most High and Jesus the Christ, to glorify his holy one."

The assembly worshipped God, jumping and shouting.

"Lyricist, reveal the Word of God."

A little man, maybe four-feet-tall, stood before the altar of the Lord. "I read from *Revelations 19*, beginning at verse 11." He dried his tears. "Let us praise God and his Queen. La Rose, before the end of time, you will bring forth Our King for the final time." The man, although small in stature, positioned himself at the altar of the Most High, prepared, anxious and honored to pronounce the Word.

11"And I saw heaven opened, and behold a white horse; and he that sat upon him was called faithful and true, and with justice doth he judge and fight.

12And his eyes were as a flame of fire, and on his head were many diadems, and he had a name written, which no man knoweth but himself.

13And he was clothed with a garment sprinkled with blood; and his name is called The Word of God.

14And the armies that are in heaven followed him on white horses, clothed in fine linen, white and clean.

15And out of his mouth proceedeth a sharp two edged sword; that with it he may strike the nations. And he shall rule them with a rod of iron; and he treadeth the winepress of the fierceness of wrath of God the Almighty.

[16] And he hath on his garment, and on his thigh written: King of Kings and Lord of Lords.

The small man wept. "Le Baton. Our King and Savior will return to us once more. May God have mercy. May le Baton have mercy on man. But may he judge the wicked who has taken his name in vain." The small squire considered his words. "Father forgive me. May *le Baton* deal with the wicked according to your wisdom."

The assembly praised God and praised the holy mother who had returned to them once more. She would return yet again, for her time had not yet come. Even the fallen angels who despised the Most High's creation cried out, for the Lord wouldn't allow them not to.

The Black High Priest, in the white vestments, whom the holy proclaimed as Melchizedek, removed the crown from the child's head, placing it upon a pillow held by the small man standing beside him, wearing ruby red vestments. The smaller man knelt, casting his head downward.

Melchizedek removed the child from her basket and disrobed her. The child wiggled in his hands as he held her up before the assembly. "Oh Holy One of the Most High God, the blood of Christ covers you, having come from you and the Most High." He lowered the child, cradling her in his arms. A fount appeared before the altar. "I baptize you in the name of the Father, the Son, and the Holy Spirit." The man submerged the baby in the fount, bringing her out quickly. The child wept. "I shall only present you once more, before the End of Days."

Two women appeared before the assembly. Their skin was whiter than snow. Were they albino twins? Their hair was white as well. Augustus looked up from his cowered position before the altar and watched as one of the women took his child from the priest. The other dried her with a towel embroidered with iridescent silk red roses. She gave the towel to another small man who had appeared by her side. He carefully folded the towel and then disappeared.

Augustus noticed the Black man's white robe was now covered with red roses. The roses continued to materialize and bloom upon his robe.

Singing and rejoicing filled the sanctuary.

Augustus wept.

His little one stopped crying, wearing her little burlap shift once again. One of the twins returned her to the man wearing once white robe, now covered with roses. He placed her in the wicker basket and replaced the crown upon her head.

Lawrence appeared before the assembly in a golden robe, embroidered with red roses as well. A Chinese man approached the altar and faced him with his long, white mustache trailing behind him. Augustus heard the name Li Zhan. Augustus had seen him before, but couldn't remember where. The Chinese man's robe was constructed of a green silk, more brilliant than the finest emeralds on earth. A jade altar adorned the breast of his robe. The men bowed to each other. Doing an about face, the Chinese man departed, coming to a halt beside Emmanuel.

A tall Black man in royal garb entered the room, soaring to a height taller than any person present, clothed in a garment spun of gold threads. *I know him,* Augustus told himself. He saw the name 'Albertus' float above he man's head and then disappear. He wondered if he ever saw it, maybe it was just his imagination. Augustus found him to be magnificent, forgetting his innate hatred of peoples different from himself.

Albertus placed three solid gold coins in the Rose's wicker basket. The congregation arose from the seats and approached the altar, fallen angels and holy alike, each dropping identical gold coins on the altar before the infant's basket. The coins spilled to the floor, overflowing, soaring into a mountain exceeding width and height of any upon the earth. The wealth of Augustus' little one's throne exceeded anything which could be imagined by man, for God had made it so.

The Ark of the Covenant appeared in Albertus' hands,

dwarfed to the size of a miniature against his gigantic physique. He sat the enormous Ark before the altar. It glowed white hot. The lid opened, releasing a Spirit no man, angel, or devil could withstand. The Holy Spirit filled the room. The worshippers swooned.

After a time, all present regained their wits. Lawrence smiled at Augustus and Sammie. Three men he didn't know began to sing in his native French tongue. He saw names appear above their heads, Louis, Jeffery and Maurice. A choir appeared, accenting the praise. A censer materialized in Lawrence's hand, which he swung to and fro, releasing its incense, which filled the sanctuary. The fragrance of frankincense sedated Augustus and Sammie. Sammie swooned into Augustus' arms, overcome. He found himself barely able to support her and maintain his own faculties at the same time.

Sammie cried without restraint, praising God and praying for the welfare of her little one, for she would overcome many trials throughout the course of her life. Lawrence continued to swing the censer back and forth three additional times. The sanctuary filled with a bright light, blinding both Augustus and Sammie.

I present to you, my Rose

AUGUSTUS SAT UP in Sammie's bed. He shook Sammie. "Where's Lela?"

Sammie awoke from her slumber, terrified. She looked in the basket, sitting on the floor, finding Lela asleep inside. Getting out of bed, she removed her child from her basket without awakening her. Sammie placed her lips on the child's forehead, and then her nose to the child's cheek. "She's fine," Sammie said in a whisper, relieved. "Gus?"

"What?"

"I dreamed I'se couldn't find her."

Augustus became prickly all over. "Well, she's fine. Go on back to sleep." He laid down and closed his eyes.

Sammie placed her child beside her in the bed, keeping her close. However, she couldn't fall asleep, still troubled by her dream. Although she had lost her child, she had found her sitting on a throne. Sammie fretted, trying to remember the fading dream. Had it been a throne? She looked out the small opaque window of her cabin, trying to remember.

Augustus lay beside her, unable to sleep. Although he didn't tell Sammie, he also had a dream. All had bowed down to worship his baby girl. He hardened his heart and cursed the dream. Nothing holy could come from him.

New Orleans, Louisiana. August 28, 1963

ONCE AGAIN, HIS grandmère had left him speechless. He didn't even know how to address what she had just shared with him. *I am the Queen.* Her earlier words rang in his ears. He turned to her, but she returned his gaze without saying anything. It was as if she was waiting for him to reach his own conclusions. He said nothing. *That's impossible*, he said in his heart. Lela stared at him, her eyes blank, revealing nothing. She frightened him at times. He stared at her a few moments more, trying to make sense of it all. He couldn't figure it out.

Julian allowed himself to imagine what it must have been like for Augustus to learn of Sammie's pregnancy. He could see Augustus sitting on the porch of Sammie's cabin with baby Lela on his knee, perfect in every way. Maybe he bounced her on his knee and the child would smile at him. He could see Augustus with the child in his library once she became a little older, propped up on the sofa. Maybe Lawrence would come in and play with her, bringing with him sweet treats and fruit. Augustus probably would have allowed it, proud of his little daughter.

Julian frowned, thinking of what it would have been like for Augustus, when he desired to take the child to town to parade her before the townspeople. He could never do that. Everyone would've known she was Black.

Lela watched her grandson's brow furrow in rage and shame. Even now, it still hurt. "You're right, Julian," she said to him.

"Right about what?"

"Augustus was proud of me. He loved me, at first. He was very proud of me, but ashamed at the same time. It enraged him he couldn't present me to the world, for everyone would've known his sin. It was a joyous, yet a difficult time for him." Lela sighed, thinking. She looked over the tree line into the past. "Maybe if he hadn't alienated his father, Emmanuel, he could have helped Augustus by providing him with a solution to his dilemma. But Father wasn't one to ask for help. He would rather destroy everything around him than to ask for help." Lela scratched her head with one finger, careful not to muss her hair. She allowed the matter to rest. "Besides, Augustus had bigger problems other than my existence."

"Like what?"

"His daughter, Lily." Sorrow overcame Lela.

Chapter 11

His cigar order had finally arrived. Anxious to sample them, Augustus rode Rock to Amite to get a box. He could have sent one of the boys, but he wanted to get out for a bit.

Dismounting and tying Rock to the rail, the men sitting on the porch of the general store stared at him. He tipped his hat to them and continued on his way inside.

Augustus waited at the counter for Mr. Howard, the owner of the general store, to return. He heard laughter wander inside from the porch. The men hushed themselves. He heard laughter erupt again. Augustus had the feeling they were laughing at him. Jealous, broke ass motherfuckers. He would own them all within the year.

"Here's a box of your cigars, Mr. Chevalier," Mr. Howard said as he exited the store room. "Did you bring your wagon?"

"Naw. I'll send one of the boys to fetch the cases. Just

needed something to tie me over until then," Augustus said. The men laughed. He actually liked Mr. Howard. He wasn't an ass kisser. Augustus heard the men outside laugh again. "What's so funny?"

"I'm not sure. They've been pretty quiet all morning," Howard said. Then his face sagged.

"What is it?"

Mr. Howard hesitated. He remembered the rumor of how Augustus had beat Suthers to death for bragging about his own relations with Augustus' wife, Emmie Sue, in their youth. "I'se don't care for gossip, or to gossip 'bout others. It never comes to any good." Mr. Howard heard the men laugh again. He winked at Augustus. "Why don't you come out back with me, Mr. Chevalier? I have some things to show you," Mr. Howard said, loud enough for the men outdoors to hear.

"Alright." However, instead of following Mr. Howard, Augustus stood inside the door, out of sight. He heard the men talking, a little louder now, about Lily. "Little red-haired bastard," one of the men said. "I'll never allow that fellow to doctor on my wife, that's fo' sure," another said. The men burst into laughter once again.

Augustus exploded through the door. He found one of the men sitting with his legs outstretched, leaned back in his chair. Augustus brought his booted foot down on his shins, breaking both of his legs at once. The man screamed in agony. He grabbed another by the neck, attempting to snap it. One of the young boys ran off. The third man pulled a gun as Augustus pulled his pistol on him. "I betcha I'll lay you out on this porch before you can pull that trigger." The man put his gun away. Augustus left the porch and mounted Rock.

"You ain't going nowhere, Mr. Chevalier," the sheriff told him with shaving cream on his face. The young boy who had run off to fetch him stood at the sheriff's side.

Augustus frowned and then a sinister smile adorned him. Just his luck the sheriff was next door at the barber's. "Watch me."

HE BURNED WITH fury by the time he reached La Rose. Augustus had to pay the sheriff one hundred dollars in gold to forget the incident and release him. The sheriff had sent his deputy to fetch Mr. Caprieze to open the bank. Augustus had followed him into the bank's safe to the Chevalier vault. He didn't go into his large vault, but opted to open one of the smaller drawers outside the vault to retrieve the bail money. He paid the sheriff and left.

The victim's wife had cried murder. Augustus refused to pay her one dime to compensate her for husband's crippled legs. "Let her get her pay out of the sheriff," he muttered as he popped the reigns. Rock bolted into full gallop up the hill to the house, energized by Augustus' rage.

Running into the house, he went straight to her sitting room. He punched her. Augustus couldn't stop beating Emmie Sue, consumed with hatred for her. He punched her again. "You're turning me into the parish fool with that red-haired gal. She looks more and more like your doctor every day," he said, bellowing so loud the servants could hear.

"Augustus, she's yours. Why do you listen to them?" Emmie Sue sobbed while shielding herself from his continuous blows. "I'm your wife! We had sex."

Augustus punched his wife in her mouth, knocking her to the floor. She lay before him and wept. "Yeah, you came into me to cover your sins!" His chest heaved, wishing to kick her; however, he restrained himself.

"We're even Emmie Sue. You got your little doctor to attend to your various ailments and I got the cook to feed me. You got Lily out of your deal with Marion and I got Lela with Sammie. So shut your fucking mouth and stop worryin' me with all your crying." Augustus left her lying on the sitting room floor, bloody and bleeding. He entered his library, poured himself a drink, and then sat in his chair. His thoughts swirled with insult and rage. Why did he have to endure such humiliation? Emmie Sue's continued wailing infuriated him even more. He could still hear her wailing in her sitting room.

Unable to endure her raucous any longer, he returned to her sitting room with his drink in his hand. He found Emmie Sue on the floor where he'd left her. She sat up to face him, her face swollen. Her eyes pleaded for his mercy and confidence in her testimony.

He slapped her. "Shut up!" Augustus finished his drink, indifferent to his wife's cries.

Emmie Sue quieted herself. Once she stopped crying, Emmie Sue realized he had confessed that Lela was his daughter. She'd always known the fact in her heart, but had refused to acknowledge the blatant reality of the slave girl's paternity. *Lela is his child.* The truth resonated within her mind. Jealousy spiked inside of her. No wonder Augustus doted on the child. He clothed her as well as, if not better, than Lily.

Emmie Sue stared at him in disbelief. She wished to lash out at Augustus, to beat him. But she had to consider Lily's future. How could he be angry at her about Lily? But she knew Augustus held the power. He could do as he wished, not only because he was the master of the house, but because he was a man. Men held a freedom women could only dream of.

Emmie Sue continued to confess her truth to him. She

feared Augustus might kill her child if he didn't believe her to be his. "Lily is yours," she said, pleading with him. "She looks just like you, Augustus! She has your nose, your lips. She even has the crooked little toe you do. How can you deny her?"

He stared at her, the lowest form of filth on Earth. He considered her words for a moment. The child did have his toe; but then again, they did share common ancestors. It proved nothing. Augustus succumbed to his urge to kick her.

Emmie Sue's face sagged. Clutching her side, she crawled off in despair. For she now understood, without any doubt, he would never believe her. Lily's uncanny resemblance to Marion had convicted her. Emmie Sue buried her face in the Aubusson rug and wept.

"Maybe your vision is blurred, but I can see clearly, whore," Augustus said. "She ain't mine." He left the house.

Chapter 12

Lela

After that day, Father focused his attention on me even more. Talk continued to ricochet around the parish about Ma'Dame's infidelity and her love child, Lily. Father didn't go out much while the rumors ran rampant. It was best, for he would have killed someone.

I now know my father loved me. I had forgotten his love, until this very moment. In those days, Maman would make a little palette on the floor for me in her cabin, beside her bed. She would always say, "Lela, you'se need to learn to comfort yourself and sleep alone." I didn't understand her words then, but I do now.

In any case, Father would sleep with Maman more nights than not. When they would settle into bed and I believed them to be asleep, I would go to the edge of the bed where Father slept and tickle his nose. Then I would twirl his curly hair between my fingers, creating tight locks. Once I saw him smile, but he still pretended to be asleep, frowning. I would twitch his nose again.

"Whatcha doin' gal?" I would stand before him afraid, but excited at the same time. He would then open his eyes with a frown on his face. "You cain't sleep?" I would stand before him silent, pouting a bit. I would tell him I was cold. He would grunt and say, "Git in, gal." I would jump into the bed, crawling over him, burrowing myself in between him and Maman. Maman would wrap her arm around us both, shielding me from every terror of the night. Father would turn in the bed and face Maman, cocooning me between them both. I would fall asleep, believing myself to be the most loved child in the world.

Maman would fall asleep after a time, surrendering to Father's protection. He never said anything during those nights. He loved me then. He loved us both.

In the morning, I would awake on my palette. Looking back, Maman probably placed me there once Father awoke and left. We continued in our love until I was about five or six years old.

I'm not sure why I shared this with you. I guess I wished for you to understand that even though my Father was monstrous to me during my latter years, he once loved me. He did have the capacity for love. Hard to believe, but true. He loved me in his imperfection.

In any case, Maman decided to take advantage of Father's favor on me. He had always been kind to me, but after his fight with Ma'Dame, he clung to me even more. Looking back, I wonder why he hadn't taken more interest in Jean Charles. He never seemed to care for my brother much. I think he saw him as weak. I believe he wanted a son more like himself, callous and cruel. Jean Charles was neither. Augustus had sent him away to boarding school once he turned eight years old, so he wasn't at La Rose during those times. He probably would've sold Jean Charles if he had been his slave.

Maman began to nag Father about sending me away to boarding school. He refused outright, but his protests didn't stop Maman. She had ways of dealing with Father no one on the plantation could understand. Yet, he still wouldn't allow me to go, claiming I was too young. When Maman persisted, he would yell at her, telling her he owned me and could do with me as he pleased. Maman would leave him alone for a week or so. Then she would start up with him again about me going to school. She wanted me to go to France. Augustus had no desire to send me there. But as the years went on, he began to consider the option.

La Rose Plantation. 1853

AUGUSTUS CAME INDOORS, irritated. Sammie continued to pester him about sending Lela away to school. The gal was only six years old, still too young to even attend school. Well, she would've been old enough for school in Louisiana, if she was White. Anyway, he didn't care to send her to France to attend school at her age. What if something happened to her?

Augustus sneered, realizing he cared for the child more than he should. Once he had a dream that he, Sammie, and Lela lived in France. He remembered walking along a tree lined path. Lela had been a baby in the dream. He pushed her carriage while walking arm in arm with Sammie.

He rejected the idiotic dream. He needed a drink.

Hen pecked and tired, Augustus went to his library and poured himself a drink. He sat down, trying to figure out what to do. It wouldn't be a bad idea to send Lela overseas. He wouldn't have to keep her in the house all the time. She could grow up to be a lady. It wasn't as if anyone could really tell she was a Nigger, so she might do well there. He could visit her in France. He could be her father there. He smiled to himself a bit.

Augustus pushed the fantasy out of his mind. He didn't believe in delusions of that sort. Someone would find out about her and he couldn't allow that. Augustus took a swig of bourbon as his rage mounted. No one would even know about her if it wasn't for stupid little Lily. The child had gone around town talking about a sister no one had knowledge of. Dumb little bitch. He knew it would all blow up in his face. Maybe he should listen to Sammie.

Augustus left his library and entered the foyer. He spotted Lawrence polishing the golden hall clock. "Lawrence?"

"Oui, Mis'sur?"

Augustus bit his tongue, but he had to ask. The bourbon had to ask, not him. "What do you know about schools for girls in France?"

Lawrence stopped polishing the grandfather clock, constructed of gold, and turned to him with a sly grin on his face. "As you would say Mis'sur, 'I'se just a Niggah workin' in your house.' Why'se you'se askin' me?"

Infuriated, Augustus turned to leave.

"Wait, Mis'sur."

Augustus stopped.

"Who you wanna send to school?"

Augustus turned red and wouldn't answer.

Lawrence sighed. "There's a little ole school near your family's château in Fargniers. Chevalier girls done attended the school for centuries. You'se can send a note to the butler at ya'll family's château. I'se thank Jeffrey Dupuis is his name. You'se can send your note to him."

Red-faced, Augustus nodded and returned to his library.

New Orleans, Louisiana. August 28, 1963

AFTER FIVE MINUTES of silence, Julian turned to his great-grandmother. She sat beside him with a look of awe covering her ashen face. "What's wrong with you?"

Lela turned to him. "He tried to send me away."

"Yeah, that's what you said Grandmère," Julian said, not understanding what the big deal was. "You act like you didn't know."

"I didn't."

Freak. "What do you mean, you didn't know? How can you tell me about it if you didn't already know?"

Lela took her great-grandson's hand in hers. "Darling, much of this I am learning for the first time. I wasn't aware of it before now." Lela's eyes welled with tears. "Father tried to save me, well rather save himself. He tried to save us both. I never knew it." A little dove landed on the coffee table, chirped at Lela and flew away. "I never believed he wished to educate me or that he even loved me, until today."

"He's still a racist asshole."

"Yes, he is," Lela said. "But, he was my father and he cared for me," Lela said with a smile. "At least he did for a time."

La Rose Plantation. 1853

GO ON TO the house then, Lela." Sammie watched as her little girl scurried out the kitchen door, running at full speed to their little house.

Sammie sighed as she heaped a few more coals atop the Dutch oven. Her daughter had changed, and she couldn't understand why. She seemed jumpy and skittish. She cowered when others made abrupt movements. She'd called for her sister Sarah, but she had failed to appear. Usually, she could just think of Sarah in passing and she would show up. Even her husband Teddy hadn't seen Sarah. Her little son Toot had turned up missing too. Everyone assumed his mother had taken him with her.

"Pour me a bourbon," Augustus said. He sat at the table. Sammie poured his drink and sat it before him. He looked at her and noticed her red color. He hadn't believed Niggers as dark as Sammie could turn red. "What's wrong with you, gal?"

Sammie wiped away her tears with her apron. "Somethin's wrong with Lela."

Augustus raised an eyebrow as he finished his bourbon. "What? She seems fine to me. Ain't nothing wrong with that gal."

Sammie nodded and returned to the fireplace. She raked the coals off the Dutch oven and moved it away from the heat.

"Why you think something's wrong with her?"

Sammie sat at the table with Augustus. She looked him in the eye. "My towel slid offa the table this morning. I'se jerks to catch it 'fore it could hit the floor. Lela covers her face, likes she was protectin' herself."

The hairs stood up on the back of his neck. "What?"

"You'se been beatin' her, Augustus?"

He stared at her in disbelief. "Have I been beating you?" Sammie looked away. "You talk to her?"

"She tells me ain't nothin' wrong." Sammie began to cry.

"Stop crying." He rubbed her neck and left the kitchen. Sammie returned to her work.

LILY'S CONTINUED STORIES about the mysterious sister no one had ever seen prompted several unexpected and uninvited visits from neighbors. Augustus knew the only reason for their visits was to catch a glimpse of Lily's 'sister.' As soon as he would hear Lawrence open the door and the sound of a woman's voice, he would search the house for Lela. She wasn't hard to find, usually playing with Lily in her room. He would take her to Sammie's house, commanding her not to leave.

Engrossed in his newspaper, a knock at the parlor door

startled him. His heart raced. Emmie Sue looked up from her needle point. "What is it, Lawrence?"

"Mrs. Warren has come to call with her daughter, Ma'Dame Chevalier," he said, distressed.

Augustus sat before Lawrence immobilized. The world had stopped, freezing everyone in the moment of time. Augustus recovered control of his world without delay and frowned at Lawrence. "Send that bitch home." Emmie Sue rushed from the parlor. "Emmie Sue, bring your ass back here," he said, but it was too late. She had received Mrs. Warren. He could hear his wife in the foyer, sending orders to the kitchen to have refreshments brought in.

Augustus darted out the door, brushing past Mrs. Warren without speaking and went upstairs to Lily's room. The girls weren't there. He searched every room on the second floor, finding each one empty. He even went to the third floor and the attic, finding no one. "Maybe they're outside," he said. Augustus trudged down the stairs and to the parlor, finding the women. He joined them, sitting in his wing chair.

Mrs. Warren sat on the sofa with her daughter. Just then, Sammie brought in some refreshments for them. Augustus watched as Mrs. Warren's gaze followed Sammie.

Mrs. Warren's daughter Penelope, Lily's schoolmate, sat on the sofa beside her mother. Augustus didn't care for the child. He watched her scarf down three teacakes. Little pig.

After small talk between the women ended, Mrs. Warren sat in the lavish parlor admiring its grandeur. The rumors regarding the wealth of the Chevaliers were true. She knew they owned the better part of the parish, but surely wealth of this magnitude didn't come from farming alone. She believed she'd heard the family had come from France and were of aristocratic stock.

The grand portraits gracing the parlor walls seemed to confirm it. One portrait in particular amazed her. It had to be twelve feet tall, encased in an ornate gold gilded frame. She looked into the eyes of flamboyant man wearing a powder wig. He wore a brocade coat with a ruffled shirt, knee pants, stockings, and red, high-heeled shoes. In the pastoral scene, women lounged on the lawn. Roses grew at his feet. In the background, she noticed gentle hills, with a large home constructed of stone in the distance. She had never seen anything like it. The man smiled. In fact, the man seemed to stare at her. Her eyes locked with the man in the portrait. She felt chills course throughout her body.

Mrs. Warren inhaled sharply, causing her to break her gaze with the man in the portrait. "Honey, are you alright?" Emmie Sue asked. "Aren't you feeling well, sugar?"

"What's wrong Mama?" Penelope popped another teacake in her mouth.

Lawrence appeared, handing Mrs. Warren a glass of water. Unable to speak, she looked up at the very tall Negro. He smiled at her and then left the room. He had the same smile as the man in the portrait. She sipped the water, and then losing control, gulped it down. Emmie Sue gave Mrs. Warren a handkerchief to blot her forehead. "Do you want a cold towel for your head?"

"No, Mrs. Chevalier," Mrs. Warren said just above a whisper. "I'm not sure what came over me." Emmie Sue left her place and retrieved the water pitcher from the buffet. She rushed over to where Mrs. Warren sat and refilled her glass. She drank it, slower than before, allowing the water to revitalize her. Her strength returned. Mrs. Warren noticed Mr. Chevalier glaring at her. Was he upset because she'd become ill?

Having recovered, she remembered her little daughter. "Would it be alright if Penelope went upstairs to play with Lily?"

"Why, that's a fine idea," Emmie Sue said. "I'll have Lawrence take her."

Penelope clapped her hands together. "Oh Mama! I finally get to meet Lily's sister," she said once Emmie Sue left the parlor.

"Lily doesn't have a sister," Augustus said. Now everyone would know. He couldn't stop it from happening. But he could. Augustus bolted from his chair, headed upstairs to search for the girls once more, but Emmie Sue and Lawrence blocked his path.

"Penelope, go with Lawrence. He will take you to Lily," Emmie Sue said.

The girl followed him. Augustus turned red and returned to his chair in the parlor.

Mrs. Warren smiled. "Why Emmie Sue, you never told me!"

She stared at the woman, confused. "Told you what, honey?"

"That you had another child. How could I have missed that?" Mrs. Warren felt a little embarrassed and bewildered.

"Of course, I have another child. I have Jean Charles."

Mrs. Warren's confusion intensified. "You don't have another daughter?"

"No, of course not. Why would you ask such a thing?"

The women's chatter droned on in the background of Augustus' terror. Penelope never returned to the parlor, so she must have located Lily and Lela. He began to sweat. After fifteen minutes, the adults could hear little feet pattering about above them.

Mrs. Warren rushed out of the parlor and stood in the center of the foyer, looking upstairs to the second floor in search of her daughter. Yet, she became distracted by the home's architecture and the opulence of its interior. Why hadn't she noticed when she entered? Mrs. Warren marveled at the grand, white marble central staircase ascending from the foyer to a grand landing, from there separating into a white marble bifurcated stair, coming to rest on either side of the foyer. Rose adorned gold balusters supported the gold handrails. The pattern continued around the perimeter of the second-floor walkway. Who possessed gold handrails? Perhaps they were brass, Mrs. Warren concluded.

A series of gold, Corinthian columns on the first floor supported the walkway above, creating a breezy colonnade below. Without warning, the stained-glass dome within the ceiling above commandeered her attention, depicting a country scene with the largest rose blossom she'd ever seen at its center.

Mrs. Warren redirected her attention from the mansion's stunning interior to her daughter and her playmates. She spotted a pretty little girl chasing the older girls. "You were pulling my leg—" Mrs. Warren fell silent, staring at the child. She was a little doll, a miniature female version of Augustus, well attired. Something was off about the child's appearance. Mrs. Warren caught a good look at the child's face. Her nose was different. It should have been a bit keener. She turned to examine Emmie Sue and Augustus. Their noses were sleeker, more narrow and prominent. She turned red.

Nigger

"Penelope! Come along. It's time for us to leave," she said to her daughter.

"But Ma—"

"Come, now," Mrs. Warren said in a shout, but then calmed herself. She removed her gloves from her handbag and put them on. "Thank you for welcoming us into your home, Mrs. Chevalier. I apologize we must leave so soon, but we have others to call on before supper time."

Emmie Sue cast her eyes down a bit, focusing on Mrs. Warren buttoning her glove. "Well of course. I understand. Maybe I'll call on you next time."

Penelope appeared at her mother's side. She took her hand, disappointed. Lawrence entered the foyer, handing the woman and her child their parasols. "Perhaps. Good morning to you both, Mr. and Mrs. Chevalier."

Lawrence closed the door behind them. Emmie Sue ran upstairs to her bedroom and shut the door. Lily and Lela stood on the second floor, not understanding why their friend had left so soon. "Come on, Lela," Lily said, returning to her room.

Lela tarried at the banister, looking down at her father for love, reassurance, and approval. Her father scowled at her. She turned and followed Lily.

Augustus went to his library and poured himself a bourbon. He noticed an envelope sitting on his desk. He read the return address.

Monsieur Jeffrey Dupuis
Fargniers, France.

Tears rolled down his face against his will. Augustus turned the unopened letter about between his fingers. He picked up his crystal desk lighter, lit the letter, and placed it in the ashtray. "Now it comes, after three months." Augustus watched it burn. Once consumed, he left his desk and sat in his wing chair. He stared at the floor, burning with hatred. Lela had become a shameful thing to him.

Chapter 13

La Rose Plantation, 1853

Augustus woke up, damp with bourbon. "Dammit," he said. He must have dozed off and split his drink.

He had been drinking steadily since Mrs. Warren's visit a few months before, trying to forget the look of disgust and disdain on her face. He should kill her. How dare she look down on him or anything in his house. Her family was only one bad crop away from returning to their former status as the parish's poor White trash.

Augustus heard something crash upstairs, muffled cries, and feet rushing about. He went into the hallway to find Lawrence standing at the base of the stairs grasping the angel atop the newel post. "What's going on up there?"

Lawrence wiped away his tears. "You'se should go and find out. Ma'Dame don't know you'se here. She thanks you'se in town," Lawrence said and walked away.

Augustus went upstairs and then to the rear of the

house, where Lela slept. There was a little room back there Lawrence had fixed up for her. He opened the door.

Emmie Sue grunted as she repeatedly struck Lela. Lela lay motionless on the floor, gritting her teeth. Before Augustus' eyes, a welt sprung up across her face, where the leather belt had kissed her.

Emmie Sue raised the leather belt to strike her again. Augustus grabbed the tail when it flew up and over her shoulder. He bound Emmie Sue with the belt and then covered her mouth before she could scream.

"Go to your Maman's, Lela." Lela lay before him, motionless. "Lawrence!" Lawrence appeared in the small room. He rushed in and carried Lela away.

Augustus kicked the door closed. He pinned Emmie Sue to the wall, still bound within the belt's grip. Augustus caressed Emmie Sue's neck with his nose, inhaling her fragrance. Gardenias. "Didn't think I'd catch you, huh?" Augustus exhaled his bourbon laden breath into her face, his adrenaline racing his body. He ran his finger down her cheek. She was breathing so hard, her chest rising up and down. It confused him for a moment. Drawn back to her neck, he sniffed her, savoring her fear mingling with her pheromones and perfume. Gardenia, sex, and terror were complimentary notes comprising her animalistic perfume.

Augustus lifted her from the floor. Too many petticoats.

He unbuttoned his fly. "Just once more, for the good times?" He grimaced, managing the passion raging inside of him. "Yes, Emmie Sue?"

SHE SOUNDED LIKE a sack of wet sugar.

He looked over the banister, down into the foyer. Was she dead? He wasn't sure at first. Then he saw blood pool around her head. Emmie Sue had hit the floor head first. Augustus restrained his impulse to jump up and down. The bitch was dead. Lying bitch. Then beating Lela like a dog? He wondered how long she had been beating her. Probably since that Warren bitch came to call. "No, before then," he said, remembering his conversation with Sammie months before regarding the change in Lela's behavior.

Emmie Sue was in a better place now. No one in Amite would talk to her anyway. In fact, they'd both been ostracized. Worn out from a long day, Augustus retired for the evening, at peace.

Lela

MA'DAME HAD BEEN beating me for at least two years before Father found out, even before Mrs. Warren's visit. Her beatings intensified after her visit, becoming more brutal. She would beat me for hours. I didn't even tell Maman, because Ma'Dame threatened to sell Maman off while Augustus was away if I told. So, I took the beatings. Lily saved me a few times. Her mother didn't want Lily to know she was a monster. Lily would dress and bind my wounds. Then she would tell me stories of princes in faraway lands. She would always say, "Your prince will come and save you, Lela. My prince will come too. They will save us both and take us away." I believed her.

I think we would have been alright, but people were talking, especially after Mrs. Warren's visit. Once Ma'Dame died, the gossip ballooned out of control. I'm surprised they didn't print the rumors in the newspapers. Folks around town debated if Augustus had killed his wife. Some even said he killed her because she'd been beating me. Lily hadn't help matters, crying at school because her mother was beating her sister. So, when Ma'Dame died, no one could stop talking about it.

Someone shot my father's horse, Rock, trying to kill him. They weren't a very good shot, only wounding the animal. Father had to put him down, out there on the road. Augustus escaped several close calls afterwards. It was as if an angel protected him from the repeated attempts on his life. They could never kill him. I suspect his stalker was Michael Roberts, attempting to avenge his daughter's death.

Father assumed Ma'Dame's role. He began to beat me. Looking back, I think Father beat me to prove to the townspeople I wasn't his and meant nothing to him. He would beat me in the yard. One day, he thought Maman was in the kitchen of the plantation house. He punched me in the yard. All of the slaves saw him whipping me, for no reason. Maman ran out of our little house and jumped on his back, trying to pull him off of me. He turned and punched her in her mouth. They both stopped, one staring in disbelief at the other. Apparently, he had never struck her. "You're the reason why," I heard him say. He beat Maman like a dog that day. Lawrence ran out and pulled him off her. Maman looked at him as if she didn't know him anymore.

She stood up in the little road and reached into her apron pocket. Maman removed the three little coffee beans she had kept there for close to forty years. She spat on them and then flung them at Augustus, striking him on the forehead between his eyes. The whole area turned red and oozed, burning him. Maman muttered something at him I couldn't understand. Father turned red and went to the house. Maman melted into grief and lay in the road and cried. I tugged on her hand, begging her to get up. Maman stood, wiped her face with her apron, and took me in our house.

After several years of beatings, I couldn't remember the time before Ma'Dame's death, when Father was kind to me. I would try and avoid him. But, he would always demand me to be in his presence at some point during the day. He drank more and more. He rarely went anywhere but to the whore house. For some reason, his beatings became less frequent because Lawrence wouldn't leave me unattended. I believe he feared Lawrence. I could never understand back then why he feared his Negro slave.

It always baffled me why Father cared about what the townspeople thought about him. He didn't care when they said he had murdered someone. Pretty much everyone had a Negro child somewhere in St. Helena Parish in those days; however, Augustus couldn't tolerate the thought of them believing he had one. Once I turned one hundred years old, the Lord gave me understanding about my father. I saw the truth. He didn't want those around him passing judgment on his creation. So, he decided to condemn me before they could.

Really, it was Augustus who found me less than perfect. I was Negro and he couldn't get pass it. I was Negro, so Mrs. Warren had shunned me. When she shunned me, it fell on Augustus and he couldn't endure it.

Shame is when another compels you to shun your heart's desire based on their values, what they deem as holy. They convince you that your passion and joy is less than perfect, something profane before the eyes of God. These individuals condemn your joy, convincing you to be a sin, to be evil and nasty.

Shame is a burning in your heart, a consuming flame seeking to destroy you. The flame is fueled by a lack of self-worth and confidence in your creation, mingled with the inability to forgive oneself, seasoned with conditional, unattainable, and in some cases unrequited love. I can't describe the feeling. It's something one must experience to understand. Augustus could only squelch its burning by judging his own flesh and condemning it before the world. Every time he hit me, he condemned me. It was better than someone else finding his creation less than perfect.

I remember the day when Lawrence had to run and get a ham from the smokehouse. I'm not sure where Maman was, for usually she would have done it. Augustus heard Lawrence's words as he entered the kitchen. Lawrence tried to back out of going, but he had already declared he had to go to the smokehouse. He had to fulfill his word for a reason I couldn't understand back then.

Once Lawrence left, Father almost killed me. Lawrence raced into the kitchen, for he knew I was near death. Father went to New Orleans and stayed there three months.

Chapter 14

Lela

The time had come for Lily to go away to school. My brother Jean Charles had completed his studies and had returned to plantation, not long after Father tried to kill me. I'm guessing Lawrence had sent for him, for no one knew how long Father would be gone. Someone needed to manage the plantation, so Jean Charles came home.

He loved his sister and had found an exclusive finishing school for girls, somewhere near Fargniers, France. He wished for me go with her, although I was still young. Since Father was away, Jean Charles made the decision to send me as well. I was so excited! Lily and I would sit in her room and plan our adventures in France.

Two weeks prior to our departure, Father returned. Once he discovered Jean Charles' plan to send me away, he punched him in his chest and told him I wasn't going anywhere.

I'm not sure what got into Jean Charles, but he wouldn't back down on me going to school. For the weeks which followed he argued with Father, trying to convince him to allow me to attend. Father refused. He wished for me to stay and suffer with him.

On the night of Lily's departure, Father sat in the parlor drinking, consuming two bottles of whiskey while sitting in his wing chair. He fell asleep. Once he did, Jean Charles came in and shook him, awakening him. "Papa, Lela is going to school with Lily. They leave tonight for New Orleans."

Augustus smiled. "My little girl! She's leaving me tonight?" A begrudging grin coursed across his face for a brief moment, lost in the love of his heart, the door opened by the whiskey keeper. "I'll kiss her before she goes."

Augustus passed out.

Jean Charles ran to the foyer and called us downstairs. I couldn't move very fast, still healing from my father's beating a few months before. Jean Charles hugged and kissed us both.

Lawrence put us in the carriage. Lily and I left that night.

La Rose Plantation. 1854

AUGUSTUS SEARCHED THE grounds for Lela. He saw Sarah the Slave at the well. "I know you got something to do with this, bitch."

"With what?"

"Lela disappearing. Where is she?"

Sarah laughed at him, admiring the late summer flowers blooming to the rear of the well. She drew up a bucket of cool water, and then dipped the ladle within. She sipped from the dipper and tossed out on the ground the water which remained, satisfied. "You'se a fool, Massa. You'se granted that gal permission to go to school with Lily. They probably done left the Port of New Orleans by now, headed for France."

Augustus struck her. His arm went numb and then burned like fire. "I'se ain't my sistah and I'se ain't Lela. You'se can't just beat on me."

"You stay out of my business, Sarah. They belong to me. And though you may tend to forget, you belong to me too."

"I'se belongs to the Most High, just like you'se do, my brother, my Massa."

Augustus lunged at her, but she had disappeared. He almost fell into the well.

Lela

I WAS GONE for two years. I became human. So many people visited Lily and me in France, taking us to parties, museums. They didn't seem to care I was Negro. They all introduced themselves as cousins. Giant men tucked my arm into theirs. Women of lesser stature, in some cases, adorned us both in finery. Each and every one doted upon us. I assumed, back then, they did so because of Lily.

If I remember correctly, one man named Jonathan doted on my sister. He took her on short jaunts, purchasing bobbles for her, whatever suited her fancy or his. They would take day trips together.

In the evening, Lily and I would lie in bed together and she would disclose their adventures together. I would ask her if he loved her, but she would say no. "I'm his cousin, Lela." I would nod. I could tell the man loved her, but I didn't wish to upset her perception of their relationship. If I recall correctly, there always seemed to be two men in the background of their encounters, one petite and the other of grand stature, seeming to chaperon their activities. But my sister was an innocent, never perceiving the true intentions of others, if they conflicted with her own ideals.

I remember, even now, pale, translucent skinned twin women, taking Lily and I on shopping trips, inundating us with all of the jewelry and fine clothing France had to offer. Yet, they only seemed to bow to me, ever so slightly in discreetness. They would smile and kiss Lily. She didn't seem to notice, lost in her, well our, heyday.

We sat beside one another at yet another luncheon. "Lily, you have so many relations here," I said to her. We were visiting our cousin Jonathan, yet again, in Brussels that day. He had such a grand home. It was a palace! We continued to giggle at the table. Jonathan sat beside Lily at the enormous table, able to host at least one hundred guests. The servants continued to bring in additional chairs and place settings to accommodate all the guests who continued to arrive.

Hearing our words, our host Jonathan smiled at me and said, "But Lela darling, you're our relation too. You are our family and our Queen." His comment struck me as strange. I let it go.

Now young ladies, Lily and I returned home after two years. I didn't wish to go back, but I didn't have a choice. I rushed from the carriage and to the rear of the mansion with the thick scent of pine needles accosting my lungs, anxious to greet and kiss my mother. I had dreamed of her every night of my absence, all the while ingesting the mystical aroma of roses intermingled with new peonies and pine cones.

As soon as I walked through my mother's door I found Augustus sitting in the lone chair of her humble home, waiting for me. He arose and stood before me. At first, I saw pride in his eyes, admiring me in my fine Parisian dress, adorned with jewels. *She is perfect. She is my real daughter,* I heard him say in his heart. Soon, his eyes mutated into anger and hatred. He punched me in my mouth. "Don't run off again." He left the cabin. At that moment, I wished I'd never returned.

BY HER EIGHTEENTH year, Lily had matured into a stunning young woman. She had vibrant red hair, cascading down into long soft curls. She wore it up swept much of the time, as was the fashion of the day.

Lily and I ran down the stairs from her room. We still behaved as little girls, but times were different then. We still had the minds of children. I was twelve that year. She never looked down on me because I was younger. We continued to play together, as always.

We would talk about the young men in the community and whom she considered for marriage. By the end of our analysis, her smile would fade, as the reality of her situation reclaimed her. "Let's tell stories," she would say, changing the subject.

Lily would tell me stories of princes coming to take us away to our fairy-tale futures. We would lay on her bed and dream, each relying on the stories of the other to help us endure our lives.

At times, I would find Lily in her room crying. I would run to her and ask what was wrong. She would say, "Oh, Lela. I'm just being silly." She would wipe away her tears and pull out a book to read to me. She adored Elizabeth Barrett

Browning's poems, speaking of love.

One day, she couldn't contain her heartbreak. She confessed one of her friends had told her none of the young men in the parish wished to date her, but she wouldn't tell her why.

We later learned Augustus wouldn't allow anyone to call on her. I forget how we found out. I believe my Tante Sarah told Maman and Maman told me. Lily and I would cry together, now understanding why none of the eligible young men would come to call. I would comfort her, telling her God had a special prince he would send to rescue her from Father. We would laugh about it. Then I would remind her to take me with her as her maid, once he came. She promised she would, and I believed her.

Now, in my old age, I can see how Augustus would defame her character, discouraging her potential beaus by telling them she was a bastard. He was just plain evil to Lily and she'd never done anything to him, except seek his love and acceptance. However, Father could only see her mother's betrayal every time he saw her, as if he'd been faithful to Ma'Dame Chevalier.

"LET'S GO FOR a walk."

I didn't wish to, but I had been in the house since returning from school. I could use a little sunlight. "Alright," I said to Lily.

We enjoyed the day, wandering down to the pond. After eating the lunch Maman had packed for us, we began our journey back to the house. I didn't wish to return, resolved to revel in the joy of life with my sister.

Once we reached the square, a strange man stopped us. I had never seen him before. "Bonjour, Mademoiselle Lily."

Flirtation arose in my sister's eyes. "Bonjour, Jimmy."

I wished to continue on our way, but I could sense my sister's infatuation with the boy. "Who is this, accompanying you?"

"This is my sister, Lela."

The boy considered me with a broad smile, making me uncomfortable. "It's a pleasure to make your acquaintance, Mademoiselle Lela."

He doesn't know I'm Negro, I told myself in my heart. "Bonjour," I said in a soft voice.

He took my hand and massaged it, then allowed it to fall. He walked away.

We returned the house and went to Lily's room. She seemed a little sad, but joyous at the same time. "You have an admirer."

I looked at her, confused. "What do you mean, *ma soeur?*"

Lily smoothed my rebellious hair. "You're only a child,

but you have one who loves you without concern. He's going to marry you."

"Who?"

"Jimmy."

I laughed at her. "You mean the young man we met in the square?" I slapped her on the shoulder, full of mirth. "He was only being kind."

Lily said nothing, allowing me to exist in my perception of reality.

LILY AND I left her room to forage for treats in the kitchen. Maman always left a cake or cookies in the pie safe, knowing we would want a treat in the evening. However, we didn't know if we could get there and back to Lily's room undetected by Father. "Let's take the servant stairs," Lily said. We slipped downstairs to the kitchen, unnoticed.

Lily cut two slices of cake. There was no milk, so I poured two glasses of water from the pitcher. The ice in the icebox had pretty much melted, but enough remained for our drinks. We returned up the servants' stairs, but before we reached Lily's room, the floor creaked.

"Lela, come down here and make me a drink."

Lily frowned. "Papa should be nearly drunk by now, Lela. Once he passes out, slip away. I'll wait for you, and then we can eat," Lily said. I nodded and ran downstairs.

I entered the parlor and poured my father a bourbon, setting it on the end table next to where he sat. I retreated to my designated corner. I'd left some darning work there, so I picked it up, trying to blend into the background of his world. I hoped he would pass out, but he didn't. I could see he was in a 'mood'; the bourbon talking to him. My heart beat fast.

Augustus finished the drink I'd made him. He arose from the wing chair and went to the buffet to pour himself another, forgetting to command me to make it for him. He returned to his chair, plopped down, and drank.

The glow from embers' in the fireplace dimmed, growing weaker. I watched him blink repeatedly, as if he could see things, figures I couldn't. I followed his gaze. There was nothing there but the wall. He shook his head. "Gal, put another log on."

I scurried from the corner, obeying his command. Once I placed logs on the fire and stoked it, Augustus held up his tumbler. I took it and poured him another bourbon. I placed it upon the table beside him and then returned to my darning and mending in the corner of the parlor.

Augustus gulped down his drink. He scowled, his gaze falling upon me. I could see in eyes his hatred for me. At times, I believed I could hear his thoughts and see the scenes of his life staged upon his soul, displaying before me his torments.

The sights and sounds, rather the silence of the evening began to distress me. I tried to bar the words of his heart from my mind, but I couldn't. I didn't realize back then I could hear his thoughts. I only perceived my 'sight' as an uncomfortable feeling, like when you know someone doesn't care for you, but they never tell you so. As your generation would say, Julian, I could feel his 'vibe.' To be completely honest, I believed it all to be my own imagination and paranoia.

Nigger, he said in his heart. But then he argued within I wasn't, stating I didn't look anything like Sammie. The bourbon sat before him as an unforgiving judge. Augustus continued to stare at me, momentarily abandoning his case of my racial inferiority and impurity in his heart, to exercise his hatred for his deceased wife, Emmie Sue. He called her a lying bitch.

Out of the corner of my eye I watched him scowl, having placed both me and his wife on trial before his liquor, Justice Bourbon.

His eyes grew heavy in the light of the fire. The wicks on the lamps needed to be turned up. I considered leaving my corner to turn up the lamps, but I didn't want to draw extra attention to myself. Maybe if I sat still he would pass out and I could leave the room, undetected. As if hearing my thoughts, his eyes popped opened. He reached for his tumbler sitting on the side table and finished its contents.

I could hear his thoughts again, or so I imagined. I could feel the emotion and hurt bottlenecking inside of him. He would not release it.

La Rose Plantation. 1859

HE WISHED TO cry, but refused. His whole life— What had happened? Why couldn't women ever be true? All of them had been flawed beyond repair, his Maman, Emmie Sue, and Sammie. Sammie, another Nigger. Why did he always fall for them? He frowned, and then smiled within.

She didn't fear him. A turn-on for him, her lack of fear compelled him to love her even more. Everyone feared him, Whites and Niggers alike. But she never had. Yet, her fearlessness pissed him off at the same time. Why couldn't she obey him, without all of the back talk?

If it hadn't been for Sammie, Augustus would have kept Lela hidden away. Sammie had nagged him to educate her. How she had convinced him to do so, even Augustus didn't understand. In fact, she hadn't. Oh yes, Jean Charles had tricked him. Traitor. Even his own son had betrayed him.

A tear fell as his thoughts returned to Lela. Although perfect in every way, she possessed the most devastating defect. Couldn't he have one female in his life whom he could love with his whole heart?

Finishing his drink, he walked over to the buffet to pour another. Gulping it down, he peered into the mirror above the mantle. He didn't recognize the eyes staring back at him. The voices in his head coached him, guiding him along their intended path. Justice Bourbon had reached a decision, acquitting him.

Take your freedom

Lela

I WATCHED HIM grab his shotgun from above the mantle. He checked the chambers and pumped it. Walking over to where I sat, he stood before me. I could see the torment on his face, with the latent spirit of a father submitting to the judgment of the triumphant executioner. Tears filled his eyes. "I'm tired of looking in the goddamn mirror every time I look at you, gal," he said. His hatred mingled with his unrequited love for me, and then melted into heartbreak. "Why couldn't you've been my real daughter?" For many years, I didn't believe he had actually said those words.

"Papa, no!" Lily raced into the parlor with Jean Charles close behind. How could she have known? She stood between me and the shotgun.

I heard him say, "You want to give your life for this Nigger?"

I watched from behind as her body stiffened.

"So be it."

LILY LAY IN the parlor for two days. Finally, Father called for Dr. Clemens. I'm not sure how I knew what he planned to do. I just knew. The day Dr. Clemens arrived in answer to Augustus' call, I lay hidden along the road leading to the house. Once I heard his carriage approach I revealed myself, running out into the road before his carriage. The horse stopped. I walked around to the window.

"Don't go in the house, Dr. Clemens."

He stared at me, not sure of my identity. "Who are you?"

"I'm Lily's sister." Against my will, I began to cry. "Lily's dead." Tears welled in his eyes, but he said nothing. "If you enter Mis'sur's house, he will accuse you. Don't go."

"Of what? Monsieur is ill and I must—"

"There is nothing you can do for her!" I yelled, overcome with grief for my sister. "Mis'sur isn't ill. It's a trick," I said, my anguish taking over. "Leave here and never return."

Dr. Clemens stared at me, not sure what to do.

"Listen to the child, Mis'sur."

I turned to find my Aunt Sarah standing behind me, smoking a corn cob pipe. "If's you'se goes in that house, you'se gonna hang for Lily's murder. Turn back and returns the way you'se done come."

Dr. Clemens sat in his carriage, mortified by the appearance of my aunt. "Where should I go?"

"Do you have money for the boat?"

"Why yes, I have some," he said.

"Go to France. Don't come back to Louisiana 'til you'se see Lela again. She's gonna need you in that time. Augustus will be dead by then."

We both stared at her in confusion. She walked off into the brush, disappearing from sight. Weeping, Dr. Clemens ordered the driver to turn around. I didn't see him again for many years.

Chapter 15

New Orleans, Louisiana. August 28, 1963

Lela sobbed uncontrollably. Julian watched as she cradled a pillow in her arms, apologizing to it in French. Was she cuddling her dead sister in her mind? Julian said nothing, listening. Suddenly, the vision released her. She leaned back in the swing and wept. After a few moments, she fell asleep.

Julian furrowed his brow. How could Augustus' wife expect him to take a child which didn't belong to him? How cruel was it for him to father a child with a slave who was the mirror image of him, but impure because she was Black?

Julian shuddered at his own thoughts. His sympathy and understanding of Augustus' predicament contradicted every fundamental philosophy and principle for which he'd fought for in the Civil Rights Movement. Lela was Augustus' child; however, she was tainted at the same time. He scowled, not sure what to feel. How could he identify with a racist who rejected his own daughter because she was half Black?

Julian ran his fingers through his hair. What was wrong with him? Augustus was a racist bastard and deserved to be hung from a tree. But as he considered the matter further, he realized he didn't disagree with many of his practices. Julian still plotted to destroy those who had humiliated and assaulted Jannette. He liked the fact that Augustus didn't take any shit off of people; he had 'facilities' to deal with those who crossed him. But how could he admire this racist motherfucker? In his mind, it was like admiring Hitler.

Julian wished he had the chance to punish the asshole once and for all. How could he be so cruel to his grandmère? Julian left his chair and paced the terrace, unable to fully hate Augustus as he should. How could an activist such as himself have compassion for a cruel slave owner such as Augustus Chevalier, regardless of the fact the evil motherfucker's blood flowed through his veins?

Julian noticed his grandmère had awakened. It seemed to have been a short nap; however, he wasn't sure how long she had been awake. He turned his focus to the lawn's manicured edge, still lost in his internal debate.

Lela sighed, understanding her child still couldn't make sense of it all. She'd hoped her recount of the time would resolve some intrinsic challenges within his spirit. At least he could now see his own ways. Lela listened to his thoughts, finding him shocked by his own feelings, which were in direct conflict with his 1960's radical convictions. Lela said nothing, leaving him to resolve it all within his own soul. She could see he would have to face some of the same challenges, once again.

Julian returned to the swing and sat. He then got up and poured himself a drink and returned to the swing and sat again. Distracted by his mind's attempts to process Augustus and his cruelty, he rose once more, grabbing his grandmère's glass. He poured her a brandy and sat it on the table beside her. He sat on the swing next to her and stared beyond the trees. He gulped down his drink.

After a time, internally debating all he had learned, his brow relaxed. He leaned back in the swing, his rational mind deadlocked with a reality he could no longer contemplate, comprehend, or condone. Julian rolled his head towards her, appearing older than his years, remorse spilling from his eyes.

Lela kissed him on the forehead and patted his cheek.

Julian's eyes turned red. He nodded. Sitting up a bit, he placed his arm around his grandmother and rocked the swing.

Lela pat her hand on the swing's arm three times. His soul had made peace with the past, seeking her forgiveness. Julian wasn't aware of what had just occurred, but she understood. She allowed it to remain unspoken between them.

It was enough for now.

The aroma of her star gazer lilies caressed her senses, relaxing her. When she'd first called for the boy, she hadn't believed it would be so simple to harness him. Julian had submitted to her. At times she didn't have to speak, for his surrender permitted her to enter his mind, placing the events of the past within his consciousness without resistance.

She considered the gifts and abilities God had blessed her with. She never could have conceptualized her calling and her current abilities as a teenager, beaten and spat upon by Augustus and his wife. In retrospect, her gifts were in place even then. Her Tante Sarah had seen her gifts. Once she'd told her, "You'se a seein' soul. You'se just don't trusts it yet." Tante Sarah's words had baffled her as a child. Yet, her words had come to pass in Lela's old age.

She roused herself and sat up a bit in the swing, resuming her journey along the bramble paths of the past. She smoothed Julian's hair.

Chapter 16

La Rose Plantation. 1861

Augustus and the Colonel staggered to the door. "Thank you, sir, for your help on this," Augustus said, slurring his words. "You're doing our family a great service."

Lawrence stood at the door with the Colonel's hat. "You've done the South a great service with your generosity, Mr. Chevalier," the Colonel said. He swayed, trying to take control of his balance. He bumped into the door, but then regained his balance. He received his hat from Lawrence. The Colonel picked up the sack of gold coins sitting on the floor at his feet. They seemed to steady him. "He won't have any trouble. I promised you." The men shook hands and the Colonel left.

Augustus watched as his sack of gold swung from the Colonel's grasp. He doubted if the Confederacy would ever see one coin. If the Colonel was smart, they wouldn't. He frowned, but it had been worth the price. Jean Charles' name wouldn't be added to the muster rolls.

"Close the door, Lawrence," Augustus said, unable to watch his gold leave with the Colonel. He returned to his library and poured himself another drink.

Augustus pondered if he had made the right decision in paying off the Colonel to keep his son out of the war. He knew Jean Charles would be shot dead as soon as he stepped one foot on the battlefield. The boy had no sense of survival or battle. He'd lost every fight he ever found himself involved in as a child. Jean Charles wasn't like him. He wasn't a fighter.

He couldn't risk his son getting killed without producing an heir. As the alcohol further inebriated him, Augustus dreamed of his grandson, yet to be conceived. He would take a stronger hand with the boy, making him tough. He laughed with pride, thinking of a child yet to come.

He had heard rumors of Jean Charles courting the Fairmont girl. He didn't care for the Fairmonts, but then again, he hated everyone. She was a pretty little thing, full of innocence.

Augustus passed out, filling with lust, considering taking the young woman's innocence for himself.

Lela

JEAN CHARLES TOOK Cindy Fairmont as his wife,

not long after Lily died. She was a tender, genteel young girl from a prominent family on a nearby plantation. I believe Jean Charles and Cindy were well suited for each other, both of them being gentle souls.

It was a beautiful, but simple wedding. Many of Cindy's friends and family attended, as would have been expected. They held the reception at Cindy's family home. Augustus didn't attend, for he had refused to bless the union.

Fairmont Grove Plantation. 1861

ONCE THE CELEBRATION wound down, Jean Charles went out on the porch with some of the men. He admired the setting sun and thanked God for blessing him with Cindy. As the sun retired for the day below the tree line, Jean Charles' gaze rested in the shadows of the trees which bordered the property. He saw a strange light and what he believed to be smoke. He walked over to investigate.

Once he arrived at the location, he found nothing. He turned to leave when a voice called to him. "Bonsoir, Jean Charles." A man stepped out of the brush, smoking a cigarette.

"Grandpère?" Jean Charles stared at the man in amazement. Although he had never met him, his father resembled the man a great deal. His father was much taller than the man, a little broader, darker, and heavier. In any case, the man looked exactly like one of his portraits which hung in the parlor of their home, minus the powdered wig, stockings and heels. He still appeared quite handsome, his brownish colored hair pulled back into a pony tail, tied back by a black velvet ribbon. Jean Charles knew within his soul the man who stood before him must be his grandfather. He had always desired to meet him.

"Oui, mon fils. It's me." Emmanuel stomped out his cigarette in the grass and hugged his grandson, who towered above him. "You have chosen a wonderful wife."

"Merci, Grandpère," Jean Charles said. "Where have you been for so many years?" Jean Charles stood before him, bashful. "I've prayed since I was a boy you would come to visit. I would sit before your portrait and talk to you. I always hoped you could hear me and would come to call."

Emmanuel smiled at his little one. "I suppose I did hear you and now I have come," he said. He stood on his toes to kiss his grandson on the forehead. Emmanuel reached into his breast pocket. "Here's my wedding gift to you and your wife. I have two acres of land in New Orleans. It's yours. Build a home there for you and your wife." Jean Charles said nothing, left speechless by the generous gift. "Listen to me. Build a home for your family. Do not dawdle."

"Yes, Grandpère," he said. "But, I don't know how to build a house. Who should I hire? I don't have any money either."

Emmanuel smiled at him. "If you like, I can handle the construction of your home. I built La Rose. I can build your home in New Orleans, if you like."

"That would be wonderful. Merci, Grandpère!"

Emmanuel regarded his son. He prayed for him. "Do you have plans for a honeymoon?"

Jean Charles shook his head no. His father had refused to grant him his inheritance, despite the fact he had married. He didn't wish to let Cindy's father know he was penniless. The Fairmonts had paid for the wedding, as well as giving him a dowry for Cindy. Jean Charles had planned to live from the money until he could get his father to release his inheritance.

Emmanuel removed a leather envelope from his breast pocket. "While on your honeymoon, visit Brussels. Call on your cousin, Jonathan Chamberie. Give him this document." Emmanuel showed him which one. "He will fund your inheritance. Don't request it of your father again. *Comprendez?*"

"Oui, Grandpère."

"Bon." Emmanuel stood on his toes to kiss his grandson, once more. "Be happy, son." Emmanuel peered into Jean Charles eyes. "Stay away from La Rose. Do not return. Your home should be ready in a few years." He gave his grandson a heavy case. "This should be enough to finance your trip to Europe." Emmanuel concealed his sorrow from his grandson. "Now return to your guests."

Lela

AUGUSTUS RESENTED JEAN Charles' marriage, for the mere fact Jean Charles trusted and cherished his wife. My father made it his mission in life to prove to my brother that women were untrustworthy, even his own kind-hearted wife.

Two years after his marriage, Jean Charles and Cindy returned to La Rose from their honeymoon. To this day, I can't understand why he came back. He risked not only his life, but Cindy's as well, returning to Louisiana in the midst of the war. Who returns to a war zone of their own volition? But my brother had. Emmanuel had given him so much money he could have lived anywhere in the world. Nevertheless, he returned. My brother lived in a dream world when it came to Father, even after witnessing Lily's murder. But thinking back, perhaps the Holy Spirit compelled him to return for me.

La Rose Plantation. November, 1863

JEAN CHARLES SOON regretted his decision to return home. Almost every night, Cindy ran to their bedroom, breathing hard and flushed red with fear. He would ask her what was the matter, but she would say nothing. Once she even told him the mansion was haunted, for she had seen a ghost in the hallway.

After some time, Jean Charles recognized what was going on around him. Entering the parlor one evening, he found his father near the fireplace, standing close to his wife. He stood before the scene in disbelief, unable to accept the truth. "Papa, what's going on in here?"

"Nothing, boy."

Fearing Augustus, Jean Charles didn't question him further. He walked over to Cindy and took her hand, leading her away without another word. As they walked up the stairs, his mind scrambled for understanding. Did Cindy want him? Were they having an affair? He opened the door to their suite, allowing Cindy to enter first.

Once inside, Cindy sat on the edge of the sofa and said nothing. Jean Charles went to the window, looking out of the sheer curtains at the moon.

Do not believe the lie

Who had spoken to him? Jean Charles looked around, seeing no one but Cindy sitting on the sofa, frightened. He gazed out the window once more at the grounds. He saw a man, smoking a cigarette. He stared at him. "Don't believe him," he seemed to say, although Jean Charles couldn't see his face, shaded by the darkness. The man threw down his cigarette, stomping it out. He turned and retreated into the piney woods, disappearing from sight.

Jean Charles left the window and sat at Cindy's side on the sofa. He took her hand in his and patted it. "Cindy."

She melted into tears, unable to say a word.

"Is Papa?"

Cindy cried harder.

"It's alright, my darling. I know. Don't worry," he said, smoothing down her hair. "I know him, as I know you. All is well. Don't worry, my love."

Cindy reclined into his arms, releasing the pain of her constant endurance of her father-in-law's improper overtures and advances. "I promise you, my love. I will take you away from here. Do you believe me?" Jean Charles clutched her to his chest, comforting her. She nodded, accepting his promise. "Do not worry."

RACING THROUGH THE house, he followed the piercing sound of her screams. They intensified with every step he took. Reaching the parlor, Jean Charles stopped at the open door, stunned by what he found upon the couch. Rage flared inside of him. Jean Charles grabbed the poker from the hearth and struck his father over the head. Unconscious, Augustus rolled off Cindy onto the floor. Jean Charles stared at him numb, watching as his curly salt and peppered locks became soaked with his own blood. He didn't know the man who lay on the floor bleeding. He understood at that moment he never had. She whimpered.

Jean Charles guided his wife from the couch. "Are you alright, darling?"

Cindy could say nothing, her eyes red and overcast with terror.

"It's alright, my love. We will leave here this night."

"Where will we go?"

Jean Charles smiled, smoothing back her tussled hair. "I was saving it for our anniversary as a surprise, but I've built a home for us in New Orleans," he said, kissing her. "Grandpère Manny gave me the land on our wedding day, instructing me to build the home for our family. He built it for us, while we were away. It should be nearly completed." He kissed her forehead, comforting her.

Looking down at his father, his anger surged. He kicked him. Losing all control he couldn't stop, punishing him for the years of heartache he'd inflicted upon them all. Jean Charles kicked him for his mother, for Lily. He had never experienced a state of complete unbridled rage in his life. Jean Charles realized his father would've been proud of him, if he himself wasn't the object of Jean Charles' violent outburst.

Cindy screamed.

"I'm sorry," he said, halting his rampage. He didn't wish to traumatize her further. "Come."

Rushing to the front door, he took her outside and sat her on the porch swing in a distant corner. He ran back indoors.

"What's happened, Massa?"

He had startled Jean Charles. "Lawrence, Papa, I mean Monsieur Augustus—"

Lawrence rubbed Jean Charles' back, soothing him. "Johnny's pulling the carriage 'round. Yo' house finished?"

"How do you know?" Jean Charles said. He sighed, allowing it to rest. Ever since he could remember, Lawrence always seemed to have knowledge of events he should know nothing about. "In a few weeks."

"Yo' grandpère got a townhouse in New Orleans. Stay there. I'se done already sent a messenger ahead to alert Maurice of ya'll coming to stay. He's the butler there. The house is on St. Ann's. Ya'll can stay there."

Weary, Jean Charles could only nod, acknowledging his instructions.

"God's with yah, boy. Doncha worry none. Now git!"

Jean Charles fled the mansion, finding a carriage awaiting them on the front drive with a team of six horses. He grabbed Cindy's hand, leading her away.

Sarah the Slave stopped him. "Ain't you taking your sister?"

"What?" Jean Charles assisted Cindy into the carriage. He'd forgotten Lela. He knew Augustus wished her dead, too. He hated them both. "Where is she?"

"Lela!" Sarah's eyes scanned the grounds for her, shouting into the darkness. Lela ran across the lawn from God only knew where.

Sarah took her niece in her arms. "Your maman wanted this for you. Now get away from this here place 'fore your daddy kills you."

"What about Maman, Tante Sarah? We must take her too."

Sarah suppressed her tears, witnessing her sister's end. "Sammie's in God's hands. Now go on now 'fore he wakes up."

Jean Charles helped Lela into the carriage and Sarah closed the door. The driver popped the reigns, driving the team of horses into the midnight, spiriting away the sad brood to their liberty. They didn't have the opportunity to pack, leaving all behind. The desperate party of three prayed they wouldn't encounter any Union soldiers along the way.

HIS FACE WAS wet; the liquid felt like syrup. Augustus sat up from the floor, navigating his way through his hazy thoughts.

Lela

Staggering, he stood to his feet and left the parlor, headed for the little white cabin behind the house. He thrust the door open to find her lying in the bed, waiting for him.

At that moment, Augustus realized he'd fallen in love with the most dangerous of the sisters. Sammie had a great power, a higher level of witchcraft than all of them. Her sisters were impotent compared to her. He should have sold her away.

"Ain't no way you'se couldda ever done it."

Augustus walked over to the bed where she lay. He got in, straddling her with his knees. "You robbed me."

"I'se saved her."

Augustus placed his hands around her neck and massaged her. She didn't flinch. "Ain't no way in hell I'se wouldda lets you kill my'se baby. You'se a fool if you believed I'se would." Sammie wouldn't break her gaze with him, convicting him, accusing him of everything she had held in her heart for the past forty years.

"What the hell wrong wit' yah, Augustus? You'se let that low life White trash bitch comes into yo' house and curse yo' child? Then, you'se believes yo' baby is trash and you'se beat her. You'se beat me. What the hell wrongs wit' you, Augustus? That bitch ain't nobody! Hell, she would still be out on the Stretch Road pickin' cotton if Warren hadn't taken pity on her and married her, but you'se lets her come into yo' house and cuss yo' child?" Sammie glared at him, reducing his soul to rubble.

"I'se expected you'se to destroy her family. But what do you do? You destroy us. Every day I'se waited for news of one of them Warrens bein' found floatin' out 'dere in the Tangipahoa River, but it never comes. You'se lets them lives?"

Augustus massaged her neck, sinking in fingers deep within, unable to endure her disappointment in him. Humiliated.

"What happened to yah? What? You'se would kills folks for lookin' at yah wrong." Sammie studied him. "I never said nothin', but I'se knew. Nobody never said nothin' to me, but I'se knows 'bout Liddy and Li'l Sis. It was none of my business. You'se would cut them bitches tongues out for talkin' 'bout me, but you'se wouldn't stand up for Lela? You'se wouldn't gut that bitch in the road for talkin' 'bout yo' flesh and blood? I cain't for the life of me understand it." Sammie tensed a bit, but she had to finish. "You'se lets 'dese folks shame yah? And for what? For what Augustus?"

He was dying. He was dead. Sammie had scolded him, and he was dead. He desired to silence her. He couldn't bare her disdain for him. He massaged her. "You sent her away."

"I'se did. Like I'se said, I ain't gonna let you kills my baby." Sammie looked into the eyes of man she no longer knew. Yet, she did. The man she saw before her seemed familiar, but she hadn't seen him for a long time. She didn't fear him. She would defeat him, even if she lost. "I'se came to this here earth to births Lela and raise her up. I'se learns her on the way to go in this here life. I'se did what I'se came here to do. Now I'se done."

Don't leave me

Augustus massaged the tissues of her neck deeper, lost in the ecstasy of it. Sammie's being tensed at first, but then she relaxed, her eyes affixed upon him in a steady gaze. Her body fell lax, yet she didn't release her grip on his soul. Her eyes remained affixed on him, now cold and still, but the fire persisted. Unforgiven.

Augustus dismounted her and left her little house.

PART III

Chapter 1

New Orleans, Louisiana. August 28, 1963

Julian believed his grandmère would hyperventilate. As he reached for the intercom to alert Suzette and Isabel, Lela held out her hand signaling for him to stop. He went to the bar and poured her a glass of water. She smiled through her torrent of tears as she received the glass. She drank it, the coolness of the liquid seeming to soothe her soul. Julian sat beside her in the swing, holding her in his arms.

"I never knew it," Lela said.

Julian held her close and kissed her cheek, rocking her. After a few moments, Lela realized Julian was crying, as if his heart had been broken. She understood. "Darling, it is well. It's over, alright?"

Julian stiffened in her arms, shocked and confused by his own grief. He removed his handkerchief from his pocket to wipe his eyes. "I'm not sure why…"

"It's alright, my love. Just sit with Grandmère for a moment and relax." Julian rocked the swing. As he did, a cool breeze came through and soothed them both. It had to be over eighty-five degrees, but the coolness of the breeze reminded him of a fall day in Washington, D.C. He remembered one day walking across Key Bridge with Jannette, returning to his Georgetown home. He could see her smiling and the joy in her heart of being with him. He was giddy as well, although he concealed it from her.

Julian blushed.

Lela smiled and patted his knee, but said nothing.

"I never saw Maman again," Lela said a little above a whisper. "Three days after arriving in New Orleans, I began to dream of Maman all the time. In my dreams, we would sit on the front porch of our little house. She would comb my hair and braid it. Maman would tell me different things: how special I was, that I would do great things. But most of all, she would tell me how much she loved me. She would tell me she loved me again and again. I dreamed of Maman for at least a year.

Lela

AFTER ONE YEAR of living in New Orleans, Augustus figured out where Jean Charles had run to. He wasted little time coming to call on us. It was a strained visit, but Augustus didn't cause any problems. He only stayed about an hour, chatting with Jean Charles about his life in New Orleans. Augustus seemed almost normal, taking a genuine interest in his son for the first time since his childhood.

I came into the library to bring in some refreshments. I was afraid to look at him. Unable to hold back my concerns any longer, I asked him the question that had troubled me for over one year. "Monsieur?"

He wouldn't look at me. Instead, he looked out of the window. "Yeah, gal?"

"How is Maman?" The words seemed supernatural as they left my mouth, suspended in another dimension of time. He didn't answer right away. Even Jean Charles turned his attention to us, awaiting his reply.

For a reason I don't understand, I looked into my father's face. He had turned red and his eyes were wet.

"Sammie's dead."

Augustus arose from his chair and left the mansion without further explanation.

New Orleans, Louisiana. January, 1875

FOLDING THE NEWSPAPER neatly, Jean Charles placed it on the corner of his Louis XV ormolu bureau plat desk. Life had become a dream for him. Leaving La Rose Plantation had proven to be the best decision of his life.

Cindy seemed to have recovered from his father's repeated attempts to violate her. Jean Charles could never understand why his father would do such a thing. Surely, normal men viewed the wives of their sons as their own flesh, but not his father. Augustus considered every breathing soul under his roof as his property, at his disposal to use as he pleased, regardless if slave or family. *Not his wife*, Jean Charles rebelled within.

His thoughts propelled him into the past to memories of his sister Lily's murder. He could still see Lela clutching her blood soaked and lifeless body in her arms, wailing. Augustus had walked away without remorse, his justice served.

He shook off the memories. Harnessing his thoughts, his mind turned to his daughter Lily, his sister's namesake. What a blessing she had proven to be in all of their lives. He laughed, remembering her birth. Cindy wouldn't allow neither him nor Lela near the infant. In time, she relinquished her control, once she'd come to trust them. Since that time, the child had matured into a beautiful young girl, her spirit encouraging them all. She had catapulted their lives into a state of utter joy, each day revealing treasures unimagined.

A thud outside the library jarred him from his revelry. Hearing nothing else, Jean Charles shook off the cold chill and removed his book from the desk drawer, issuing checks in accordance to the vendor's invoices. "One of the servants must have dropped something," he said.

Lela

I COULD NEVER get the child to go to bed. Cindy had given up once Lily turned three years old, leaving the task to me. She would say, "She'll only listen to you anyway, Lela." She seemed a bit jealous, but in a good-hearted way. Cindy could see the special bond between us, but she didn't understand it. I didn't either, at the time. Years later, I understood.

Once again, Lily presented to me the daunting challenge of cajoling her into bed. She feigned having to use the pot several times, and then she became thirsty, asking for a glass of water. Next, she requested I read to her stories about princes in faraway lands, persevering against all perils to secure the hand of their intended loves. I would weep without her knowledge on some nights, remembering my times with her Aunt Lily, my sister.

The clock chimed half past eight o'clock. I frowned at her, unwilling to tolerate any more excuses. "Bedtime Mademoiselle."

"Lela!"

"No, Lela," I said, tickling her. Lily giggled, submitting to my command. As we walked down the hall, I stopped, spotting a body lying still in the foyer. I had to create a diversion. "Mademoiselle, let us go up the rear stairs," I said as I bent over to whisper in her ear with a coy smile, engaging her in childhood devilry. "We can get some cookies and milk from the kitchen." The child squealed with delight as we raced down the hall to the kitchen.

We returned to Lily's room. She jumped into bed and I tucked her in. I placed the tray I was carrying, laden with treats, on the table beside the bed. Lily grabbed a cookie from the tray and munched it. "Thank you, Lela," she said, grabbing the glass of milk. She drank it and smiled, proudly sporting her milk mustache. "I look like Papa now!" I smiled and kissed her forehead.

"I will return soon," I told her. I smiled at her and closed the door behind myself. She didn't care, gorging herself on the sweets. After taking a few steps from her door, I broke into a panicked run, racing down the stairs to the library.

"Monsieur!" I called to him, terrified. Jean Charles bolted up from his desk and followed me. We came to dead halt in the foyer, unable to conceptualize the unbelievable lying before us.

Immobilized at first, Jean Charles regained usage of his body. "Cindy?" He touched her. Cold. Gathering her in his arms, he wept for his love, dead in the center of the foyer.

New Orleans, Louisiana. January, 1875

"THOSE FAIRMONTS HAVE always been crazy. Something was wrong with her maman, too. It was only a matter of time."

"Shut up, Papa," Jean Charles said, his rage growing inside of him. Jean Charles had grown to hate his father, but feared him at the same time. Why hadn't he died that night?

"Don't you back talk me, Jean Charles," Augustus said, snarling at his son in disgust. "I'm going to forget it, since you're grieving." He puffed on his cigar. "That gal was of loose moral character anyway. You're better off without her."

Jean Charles lunged for him, but Augustus punched him, and then hemmed his arm behind his back. "You're truly mad, aren't you?" Augustus' evil, condescending laugh filled the room. "You think you can take me, boy?"

"Stop slandering my wife!"

Augustus let him go. "I'm leaving. Mourn your whore."

Once he heard his father's carriage pull away, Jean Charles broke down and sobbed. Why would God curse him with such a father? Augustus had blessed their family with nothing but misery. He wept even more, thinking of the abuse Lela had suffered at his hand, of Lily's murder. How could he kill her?

Jean Charles had accepted long ago his father hated all his children, seeking to annihilate each of them. He peered out the window at the live oak tree. All at once, understanding of the past crashed down upon him, revealing to him the circumstances surrounding his wife's death. "Oh God, he wouldn't." His thoughts drifted back to the night they all left La Rose, over twelve years before. He remembered his father's attempted rape of his lovely one. "Papa has paid me back." Jean Charles knew it without a doubt. He bolted from the floor and rushed to the door.

Lela

RELIEF WASHED OVER me once I heard the front door slam. I ran from the kitchen to the front of the house in time to see Augustus' buggy pull away into the rue. I breathed in deep, allowing his evil spirit to leave my being.

"Lela!"

I frowned and went to the library. "Oui, Monsieur? What is it?"

He closed the door behind me. "Lela, do you think Cindy would kill herself?"

I didn't wish to become involved. I'd had enough of the Chevalier family, of its mysteries and intrigues. "Monsieur, it isn't for me to say."

"Lela, please. For once, just say what you think."

"It isn't my position..."

"Lela!"

I conceded to his pleas. "No."

He bit his lip. "Lela, was Papa here the day Cindy died?"

My heart filled with fear, realizing for the first time Cindy's death may not have been a suicide. "Monsieur, I don't know," I said, trying to remember. "I was busy with Mademoiselle and other things around the house that day. I don't recall seeing him."

He collapsed into his chair, defeated. Once again, his father had ruined his life, and he couldn't prove it. "That will be all, Lela. Merci."

New Orleans, Louisiana. September, 1875

JEAN CHARLES WEPT, melting into a sea of grief. At least they had enjoyed fourteen years of happiness together, but for it to end like this? It seemed as if his life had been a series of tragedies. First his mother's mysterious passing, and then the 'accidental' death of his sister Lily. Now this.

He couldn't figure out why Cindy would kill herself. His father had convinced him she had. Jean Charles couldn't embrace the alternate scenario of his father having killed her. Yes, suicide must be the answer. "Cindy, did they mean more to you than your own daughter?" Staring out the window at the morning sky, the question swirled within his mind. He couldn't reach an acceptable answer to the question. "My God, she's only a little girl. Didn't you even think of her?"

A small hand tugged on his leg. "Papa, Maman couldn't stay," little Lily said to him with tears in her eyes. "Please don't be mad at Maman."

Jean Charles beheld his heart standing before him.

Opening his arms, she leapt into them, father and daughter mourning the loss of their love together. Only Lily's love could erase from his mind the image of his wife lying dead in the middle of the foyer.

He couldn't understand why she would kill herself. His father had convinced him the loss of her father and brother in the war had compelled her to jump. Augustus went on to imply that an improper relationship existed amongst the three of them. Jean Charles shook off the suggestion of incest, understanding his father to be a cruel person.

Sure, the loss of her family during the war had crushed her. However, he didn't believe their deaths had devastated Cindy to the point of suicide. It had been over ten years. In fact, she had moved on. The more he mulled it all over, it just didn't make sense. Nevertheless, he couldn't accept the alternative, unacceptable scenario. Besides, Cindy adored Lily. There was no way she would leave her. The joy of her life, she took the child everywhere with her. Cindy loved them. She loved life.

Lily drifted off to sleep in his arms, although mid-morning. "*Ma chere*," he said, kissing his child on her forehead, smiling down on her. He knew Cindy's death had devastated her, yet the child fought to be strong. "You're no longer Papa's little girl. Soon you will be seven years old."

Rocking her, he slipped off to sleep, releasing the unbearable horror of his life while rallying his strength and love for his heart, Lily.

Chapter 2

Lela

I finished the dishes and ordered the kitchen. Cook was off that day, so all was left to me. Supper sat on the table, cooling. I smiled, hearing the sound of her little feet running up the stairs from the rear yard to the kitchen door. She was my little girl too, although I held my love for her in my heart, concealing it from Jean Charles. I suspected he knew, despite my deception.

Lily burst into the kitchen, bringing with her the essence of the bright, fall day. She tossed her little reader on the table, along with her slate. She always brought it home, although she had at least three slates in her room. I suspected she toted it each day to proclaim to all who saw her that she was a big girl who attended school.

Lily ran to me, hugging me around the waist. "Oh, Lela, school was wonderful today!"

"Come, sit and tell me all about it." I loved hearing about her adventures at school. I had been fortunate enough to attend school for only a short time.

"Marlene invited me to her birthday party this Saturday!"

"She did? Oh, how wonderful." Marlene was one of the most popular girls in her class. "Oh darling, I'm so happy for you." I kissed her on the forehead. My heart fluttered a bit. "My, you're warm. Aren't you feeling well?"

"Yes Lela, I am," she said. Lily ran from the kitchen and down the hall, and then up the stairs. I stared at the child for a moment, but shrugged off the feeling. I didn't pay much attention to my 'senses' back then. I dispelled it all and returned to my work.

AS THE WEEK wore on, Lily's fever intensified. At first, we believed it to be a little cold, nothing serious. However, the fever began to creep up higher and higher, accompanied by lethargy and body aches.

The morning of the party arrived and Lily went to the parlor to say goodbye to her father. He removed his spectacles, placing them on his desk. He stood beside his little one, smiling. Bending down to her, he kissed her forehead, finding her warm. "Lily, darling, I think you should stay home today."

"But Papa, I can't miss the party. Everyone will be there," she said, pleading to him with tears in her eyes. "Please Papa, just this once?"

He kissed his little girl, fussing with an errant curl. "Oui, ma chere. You may go."

She returned home floating high above the clouds from all the fun she had enjoyed at the party. I entered the parlor as Lily told her father about the games they'd played and everyone who had attended. Noticing her red face, I raced over to the child, placing my hand on her forehead. "Mon Dieu. Monsieur, she's burning up!"

Jean Charles placed his lips on her forehead. "Oh God." We raced up the stairs, Jean Charles clutching her in his arms. He put her to bed.

"Papa, I feel fine," she said, scolding us silly adults, still riding high from her afternoon with her friends. I left the room, instructing the servants to bring up the bathtub and to tote cold water from the washroom to fill it, while Jean Charles sent his servant to get the doctor.

By the time the doctor arrived, the fever had taken control of her, ravishing her little body. She was listless, her little head thrashing from one side of her wet, sweat soaked pillow to the other, resisting the onslaught of the invader. How could she have succumbed so quickly?

After an extensive examination, the doctor confirmed our worst fears. "Yellow Fever," he said.

Jean Charles collapsed into the chair beside his heart's

bed.

SOON, ALL NEW Orleanians began to realize their children and their elderly had become afflicted with the same symptoms. High fevers ran rampant throughout the city. This news provided us with no comfort or acceptance of Lily's plight. Heartbreak and tragedy seemed to dog us without mercy.

I watched as madness began to take hold of my brother, who clung to the irrational belief that God wouldn't allow Satan to rob him again. "It has been a week, Doctor," he said. Jean Charles applied another cold compress to her head. She had been unconscious for two days. "No. Mon Dieu, please!" Jean Charles wailed, beseeching God for mercy. The doctor said nothing.

I wept in the corner near the window. Lily was leaving me, again. "Maybe we should put her back in the bath," I said, knowing it would do no good. No one had heard me, anyway.

"Monsieur, her fever is 105 degrees." The doctor sighed. "Let's place her in the bath again."

Jean Charles lifted his heart from her wet bed, easing her into the tub of ice water. She didn't flinch. Her lifeless body lay submerged in the water for an hour. Her eyes rolled back in her head.

I continued to watch her, hoping. After some time the child opened her eyes, focusing for a few moments on a figure, a target in the distance. I followed the direction of her gaze, finding nothing there. I determined no one could see the figure but her. "Monsieur, look," I said, encouraged. I watched her focus her eyes on the target. They glowed bright, full of joy.

Lily smiled, and then exhaled. Her face fell slack.

"No!" Jean Charles screamed, frantic with horror and grief. Lily slipped away. He scooped his life out of the water, wailing.

"Monsieur, she's gone," the doctor said.

Jean Charles clutched her, rocking her, all but dead himself.

Chapter 3

Once again, we returned to La Rose to entomb Lily at the right side of her mother, near the opposite wall of the Chevalier Mausoleum. I wondered why they hadn't placed her sarcophagus beside Cindy's. They'd left a large space between them. However, I was too devastated to care. Lawrence comforted me. I thought about my own mother's grave.

After Lily's internment, Lawrence walked me over to where they'd buried Maman. Tante Sarah appeared next to me. "She saved you. You'se had to survive and she tricked yo' daddy. He woke up from that blow Jean Charles gave him. The first thang he thought 'bout was you'se getting free of him. He ran to Sammie's cabin.

Sarah wiped away her tears, hugging me close. I couldn't stop crying. "Her work was done. Doncha mourn her none. Praise her."

"We could have saved her too," I said, whimpering.

"Naw, that wasn't the Most High's plan. Thangs is as they should be," Lawrence said, comforting me.

We all stood before her grave, entwined in each other's arms. They had marked her grave. Her tombstone read 'Sammie 1805 – 1863.'

"Doncha go questioning the Most High. He knows bettah than you," Sarah said.

I didn't say anything else. I placed some roses on her grave I'd cut from the garden. "But how did she die?" They ignored me, walking away.

I lay down on my mother's grave and cried.

AFTER RETURNING TO New Orleans, each day proved worse than the previous one. It began with Jean Charles taking a drink or two before bedtime so he could sleep, or so I assumed. In fact, I didn't know about his drinking at first. Then one night, I heard bumping. I crept out of my room and looked down into the foyer. I could only see his feet. I heard weeping. Was he lying on the stairs? I rushed down to the second floor, finding him sprawled out there, drunk. "Jean Charles."

"I killed her," he said.

I didn't say anything else to him. He wouldn't have heard me anyway. "Go to bed, Monsieur," I told him, grabbing his arm. I couldn't lift him.

He began to crawl up the stairs, sobbing harder. "Why do you call me Monsieur," he said to me in his stupor. I couldn't respond. "Aren't I your brother?" He smiled. But I understood he wasn't speaking to the real me, but to me in a perfect place and time. "Maybe we can all live together now."

"Monsieur?"

He looked at me, seeming to see me in the present. He wiped his eyes. Using the wall as a brace, he stood up, staggered upstairs to his room and closed the door.

I could no longer bear to watch him. My brother engaged in the motions of the day without emotion, a puppet. He spent much of the day in his library. Monsieur Jacks would come to call with a catalogue bag in hand. What did his sort need with a catalogue bag? The more he called on Jean Charles, the less I saw of my brother. After two months, I denied Monsieur Jacks audience with Jean Charles.

A few days later, I'd retired for the evening and fell into a fitful sleep. The last time I remembered hearing the hall clock, it had chimed two o'clock in the morning. I believe I must have fallen asleep. A loud noise awoke me, propelling me to sit straight up in bed. It sounded as if someone had broken a window downstairs. Had an intruder entered? I raced down the stairs, calling for Jean Charles, but he never answered. Terrified, I ran to the cabinet and got the shot gun. I'd never fired one, but I determined I could figure it out.

Scared to death, I turned the doorknob, releasing the latch. With the barrel of the shotgun, I opened the library door. I lowered my weapon once I saw him standing next to the window with a crate in his hands. Spotting me, Jean Charles sat the crate on the floor behind his desk, out of my view.

"Some roguish boys just tossed a rock through the window," he said, looking away.

I could have cried, but why? What would it have changed? Had my brother become so desperate he would destroy the stained glass window depicting cherubim and angels in a beautiful garden, so he could get a drink?

He frowned at me, and then lowered his eyes. "Close the door, Lela."

Chapter 4

La Rose Plantation. November, 1875

Augustus slammed his tumbler on the desk, splattering bourbon all about. "Dammit!" He watched as the brown liquor soaked into the leather blotter, giving depth to its rich, black color. As the intensity of the blotter's color deepened, so did his hatred and self-loathing take a foundational root in his heart.

He attempted to stand, but lost his balance, falling back into his swivel, leather wing chair. The chair rocked with violence, tossing him about as if trying to shake some sense into him.

Or the devil out of him.

Augustus steadied himself and walked over to the buffet. Removing the stopper from the crystal decanter, adorned with roses, he poured; however, the decanter had nothing left to offer.

Fucking Sammie. How hard was it for her to keep his bar stocked? He stumbled to the door and yanked it open.

"Sammie! Come here, Nigger."

A few moments later, Lawrence entered his library with a full bottle of bourbon. With ease, he uncorked the bottle and refilled the decanter. "What? You're a bitch now, Nigger? Is your name Sammie?"

Lawrence pitied the boy. He had grown tired of his continued drunkenness. But tonight, his level of intoxication had exceeded proceeding episodes, for it was the anniversary of Sammie's death. Every year at that time, his misery heightened. However, Lawrence knew this night would prove to be harsh, for it was the twelfth year. "Nawsuh, I'se ain't." Lawrence wished to hold his tongue, but couldn't. "Sammie cain't serves yah from the grave, now can she? But I'se suppose you'se gonna make her try." Augustus flushed red, turning to the stained glass window. The roses seemed wilted upon their leaded glass canvas. "You'se sent her to the grave, now's yah wants her to come back."

Augustus removed his revolver from the drawer and pulled the trigger. The weapon misfired, burning his hand. He jumped up and ran to the bar, pouring water from the pitcher on his hand, wetting the floor. "Nawsuh, she ain't gonna be back no time soon." Lawrence looked up at the angel crowning the stain glass window's motif of roses. "Maybe's when she does return, you'se acts a little better." Lawrence stopped short of sucking his teeth. "But I 'spects yah won't. But, I'se reckons you won't chokes her to death next time, though."

"Niggah get out. Get out!" Augustus pitched his useless weapon across the empty room, finding himself alone. In an instant, he forgot Lawrence's visit, returning to his relentless grief for his lost love. "I will not…" He stumbled to the bar again and poured himself a bourbon, refusing to mourn her. He returned to his chair and sat. Rage twisted his face. The empty tumbler shattered within his hand. Augustus passed out.

The hall clock chimed three times, awakening him. The moonlight streamed in through the stained-glass window's roses, enveloping him in red light. Augustus arose from his chair, grabbed the decanter and left the library.

HE WANTED TO spit, but he didn't. He shouldn't spit on the grave of his love. Augustus' agony sank down to the depths of hell. She'd stolen Lela. She had done some sort of voodoo to convince him to consent to her education (well Jean Charles, but he was convinced Sammie had something to do with it), to subdue him to allow Lela's escape.

Both times, Sammie had waited until he was good and drunk to circumvent his will. It was her fault. "That's why you're in that grave, Sammie. You stole her from me." Why couldn't Sammie understand that Lela was his property? She was the only good thing that had come from him, but at the same time profane. His saint, his sin.

The women in his life had destroyed him. They refused to obey him. Everything would have been alright if Emmie Sue hadn't opened the door that day for the Warren woman. He'd already decided to send Lela away. It was his decision. After Warren disgraced them, he'd found the letter from the butler at his family's château in France, outlining the details of the girl's education.

Wickedness skirted his face, thinking of how he had destroyed the family after Sammie died. All of them. Mr. Warren had disappeared. Overcome with grief, Mrs. Warren drowned herself in the Tangipahoa River. Pity. He had the bank foreclose on the land the family had worked for fifty years to purchase. Augustus evicted the four remaining generations of tenants. He heard they had left the parish for destinations unknown.

Fuck them.

Mrs. Warren's little piggy daughter landed in the state orphanage. He was indifferent at first, but then he remembered the day she and her mother had come to call. The girl had taken a genuine liking to Lela. He reconsidered his judgment of her, showed her mercy, and took the child as his ward. He sent her to the boarding school in France; where he had planned to send Lela.

Why hadn't he sent Lela?

He needed to keep her close. He couldn't allow anyone to see his sin.

But who would have known of his sin in France? Hell, she was as White as he. Who would have known or cared?

Folks always seemed to find out.

Augustus couldn't work it over anymore in his mind. It was all too much. He couldn't control the events of his life; he wasn't able to stop any of it. He couldn't fix it. Augustus knelt before the simple stone marker of Sammie's grave. What Nigger got a stone marker? He ran his fingers over the craved stone.

Sammie

1805 to 1863

Stone roses adorned the top two corners of the marker. Lawrence. Somehow, Augustus knew he had something to do with Sammie having a marker worthy of a White woman. Anger surged in him, but it turned to grief. "Sammie." He bit down hard on his tongue and blood flooded his mouth. The gush surged, spilling from his mouth onto Sammie's grave. Augustus spat to the right of her grave, expelling the dark liquid.

Can you not forgive yourself?

Can you not tell her you love her, even now, my son?

"Papa?" Frantic, Augustus looked about, first to the left

and then the right. Finding no one, he scooted back against her tombstone, destroyed. Something stabbed him. He turned to find nothing, but he could feel the warm liquid coursing down his back.

You have stabbed yourself in the back. No one but you.

Augustus flushed red. He couldn't receive it. He forced down his angst and his love for Sammie, and for Lela, with bourbon.

The sky became a dark, navy blue; the light challenged the darkness.

This here's Mis'sur's cup. We'se keeps it here for him

Sammie had loved him. He was her master. She was his pet. He—

"I don't love Niggers."

Augustus stood to feet; the slave grave yard swirling before him. He noticed the graves of those whom he had sent there with his own hand. His heart hardened. No forgiveness for backstabbers.

Daylight broke over the tree line, heavy and gray, full of Armageddon's judgment. There was one more to be added to the grave yard's number. He walked towards the house.

"Nigger, you gonna die this very day."

Chapter 5

New Orleans, Louisiana. November, 1875.

Sarah lifted her little one into the wagon. Life had improved for her, now that Toussaint had returned from France. He was different, and she could see he had drunk of the cup. Her son had received his anointing. But she could see he didn't remember the occurrence. His initiation had been tucked into a safe place within his soul, waiting for him to become a man. Sarah looked out into the future. Yes, it would be many years before he recalled his initiation into the *L'Order de la Rose.*

She climbed into the wagon, sitting upon the wooden bench beside her joy. She wished to kill the one who'd sired her, but it wasn't for her to do. Another would have the pleasure. He had been allowed to ruin either the Rose or her daughter. The Lord had permitted her daughter to be chosen.

Sarah suppressed the lump in her throat and squelched the urge to ask, 'why her daughter?' But she understood why.

Satan had been allowed to infuse his Seed. She considered Claret's father further, Hanzel Johannesen. How could she curse the one who had sired her grandchild? Easy, because he was the devil. Evil and holiness had intermingled within her grandchild's soul. It was well. Sarah could see her child's holiness outweighed the evil which lurked within her. The Lord would be able to use her for his will.

She popped the reigns and her horse, Honeysuckle, initiated her lazy gait, leaving the drive of Toussaint's funeral home. Sarah hadn't been surprised when he told her he had chosen Mortuary Science as his profession. Toussaint and Teddy had prepared the dead on the La Rose plantation for years. Teddy's father, Basso, (the White folks called him Bailey) had laid out the dead as well.

She still missed Teddy. A white dove flew before the carriage, just avoiding hitting them, and then darted away. Sarah sucked in her breath. She looked over at her grandchild and suppressed her tears. Why today?

Pulling the reigns, Honeysuckle turned left at the corner. Mr. Robertson waived at them from the porch of his store. Mrs. Lewis waived at them as they passed. She could hear, in the distance, Mrs. Lewis greet Mr. Robertson as she walked up the two weather worn plank steps to the porch of the store. Mr. Robertson followed her inside to attend to her.

Sarah loved the big oak trees which shaded the street.

The coolness created by their canopy refreshed her. "Look Grandmère!" Claret, her granddaughter, pointed up to a low hanging branch. Sarah eyes fell in line with the direction in which the child pointed.

"What ya'll doin' here?" Sarah's heart beat hard. "Ya'll should be outs in dah swamp somewhere."

With her words, the honeybees left their nest. Sarah found it to be unusual for bees to make their home in such a public area, on such a low branch. However, the hive thrived there, its industrious residents streaming in and out, mining their gold.

Sarah stopped the carriage. "Why are we stopping, Grandmère?"

Sarah closed her eyes, and then opened them. The worker bees streamed forth from their factory and home, falling into ranks on either side of the hive's opening. At last, the Queen Bee exited her home, flanked by several large drones. After surveying her Queendom, she flew dead center for Sarah's head. Claret attempted to fan the bees away. "Stop child. She's coming to honor your descendant."

"What?"

Sarah ignored her child. The enormous Queen buzzed around Sarah's head three times. She came to rest on the crown of her head, nesting within her locks of hair. The drones encircled Sarah's head, forming a crown.

Sarah leaned over to kiss her terrified child; however, the child didn't flinch, although Sarah could see she feared being stung by the bees comprising her crown.

Tears rolled down Sarah's face. "Today, the Queen Bee came to you. Before you'se leave dis Earth, you'se gonna visit the Queen Bea."

Claret stared at her grandmother in confusion, not understanding her words; yet, they inflamed her heart. She felt the fire of God burn within her heart, hot, but cool. Cool fire.

Sarah popped the reigns and continued their journey. Claret turned to her grandmother, finding the bees gone. "Where did they go, Grandmère?"

"Nowhere, baby." Sarah watched the residents of the Ninth Ward go about their business. She guided her wagon down busy Marais Street. Here, they were all regular folks within their own neighborhood, with their own society, commerce, royalty, joys, and pains. Here, they weren't Niggers, just hard-working folks without others to treat them as less than human. Sarah's thoughts returned to her days of liberating folks. Now that freedom had come, she had fewer folks to deliver. The Evil One still compelled some White, Indian and Negro folks alike to keep the people enslaved. She delivered as many as she could. The Lord would reveal the persecuted and she would go and get them. She spirited away many to Canada, or wherever the Lord desired them to go.

Sarah wiped her eyes. She had trained up Claret the best she could in the short time she had been blessed with her. The child would be well. What a big girl! She couldn't believe the girl was already fourteen years old, although she still could be childlike at times. Sarah had shielded her. Now, the time had come where she couldn't protect her any longer. She would grow up, fast.

It had been fourteen years since the devil took her daughter.

Missy never recovered from Hanzel's rape. Sarah looked out into the future and saw Hanzel's end. "You'se gonna fall wit' yo' pants down," she proclaimed in the Spirit. "Yessah, you most certainly will."

It was hard for Sarah to think of her daughter locked away in the asylum. Toussaint committed Missy when Claret was eight years old. At least that's what he'd told her. Missy looked at Claret one day and saw her rapist, for the child looked just like Hanzel, only with brown skin. Missy had grabbed a knife from the counter and charged the child.

In all of her years of assisting folks in fleeing bondage, Sarah had never been as terrified as she was in that moment. Teddy stepped in between Missy and Claret, blocking her path. Missy plunged the knife into her father's heart before she could stop herself. Unable to comprehend what she'd done, Missy stood over him. Sarah watched as her daughter's remaining slivers of sanity flee her eyes.

Toussaint had only been home a short time. He grabbed Missy's hand and led her to the wagon, taking and committing her to New Orleans Insane Asylum. Toussaint returned home and prepared his father for burial. He'd told the mourners his father had died of a heart attack. Well, his heart had been wounded, Sarah reasoned. They buried him at *La Rose* in the slave cemetery, beside his father Basso.

Lord, bury me beside my love

Sarah closed her eyes, envisioning her daughter as a child, happy and gay. Well, how happy could a slave be? Yet, her child had experienced favor because of her, until the devil stole her. Her son had enjoyed favor because of his father. Not because of Teddy, but because of his father.

Toussaint's father.

Sarah sighed and turned the corner. She had sent word to the asylum to sit Missy in the yard so Claret could visit with her. She didn't want Claret inside of the place, not desiring for her baby to know how her mother existed in the confines of the home. Sarah popped the reigns. Now that she thought about it, the errand boy had failed to return with confirmation the asylum would be able to receive them.

"Maman!" Claret bounced up and down on the bench,

anxious to see her mother. "Are we really going to see her?"

Sarah turned and smiled at her grandchild. "*Oui, ma Coeur.*"

Claret stood in the wagon and jumped up and down with glee, excited about the visit. "Sit down gal!" Claret sat, her enthusiasm squelched. She bowed her head. "Grandmère isn't mad. I'se just don't want ya to git hurt. Alright?"

Claret nodded, her excitement rebounding. "Grandmère?"

"Yes, ma petite fille?"

"Where are we going to visit Maman?"

Sarah sighed. She couldn't bear to think of her little Missy. To this day, she couldn't understand how she hadn't seen it about to happen. She could see the comings and goings of men and women all over the world, but she couldn't see this maniac accosting her own child? Bad part about it, she was at home that evening. She wasn't even five hundred feet away and when bastard had brutalized her daughter.

"She livin' now wit' folks like her. She wanna git better." Sarah turned in the wagon and looked down at her little Claret. She knew the child could hear her thoughts. She was much like Sarah, except she couldn't move through the Spirit as she could. She stroked the child's cheek. "I'se just hurts for the pain yo' Maman done had to bear, my darlin', but I'se wants you to know one thang."

"Yes, Grandmère?" Claret allowed her gaze to fall to the wagon floor, shame working its evil to take hold of her heart.

Sarah placed her fingers beneath her chin, lifting her head up, her eyes hard. "Doncha ever looks down in shame ever again in yo' life. You'se hear me gal?" Claret nodded. "Good."

Sarah stared down the road a bit and then returned her attention to her grandchild. "I'se so grateful the Lawd done blessed me with you. You'se the best thang that done happened to me. You'se knows that right?" Claret nodded, internalizing her grandmother's love. "Good. Doncha ever forgets that yo' Grandmère loved you."

Claret looked up to find a man standing in the road. She became a little panicked as the wagon raced towards him, her grandmother's attention focused on her and not the road. "Grandmère, I don't think he's gonna move."

My God

Lord, are you really gonna allow this? Sarah hadn't seen him in years. He looked the same, but his black curly locks were now almost white. He had bided his time to seek his revenge. How did he even know she would come along this way at this time? But then again, she knew how. Augustus was her brother, and could see just as well as she could. He just never embraced his abilities. Barachiel had fathered them both.

I won't question the Most High

It is done

Sarah stopped the wagon and pulled the brake. "Claret, doncha move outta this wagon," Sarah said.

"Grandmère, let's just turn around and go back home," Claret said, beginning to cry. She couldn't see it, but she could feel it.

Lord she's barely fourteen years old

Sarah kissed Claret on the forehead. She couldn't stop kissing and hugging her. "Yup, you'se was worth it all, darlin'. Grandmère loves you wit' all her heart." *Ma Coeur.* "You'se my heart, child." Sarah strengthened herself.

Grandmère, please...

Sarah ignored her grandchild's pleas to her in the Spirit and hopped down from the wagon. She reached into her bosom and retrieved her corn cob pipe, placing it in her mouth. She struck a match on the bottom of her shoe. The flame flared up a foot into the heavens, and then settled down. She lit her pipe, drawing on it slowly, inhaling and savoring its goodness. Sarah relaxed and strengthened herself. She turned back and looked to her heart once more. Sarah smiled, hoping to reassure her. She knew she hadn't, seeing the terror in the child's eyes. She blew her a kiss.

Sarah tilted her straw hat forward to shade her eyes and then walked towards her brother, her lifelong adversary.

People began to gather on either side of the street.

"Nigger, I told you back then you would have to atone for your sins with me one day, didn't I?"

Sarah traced a circle in the dirt road with the toe of her shoe. "Yessah, you'se did, Massa. And I'se told you yo' family would crumble and you'se would die if you split my blood."

Augustus stood before her, indifferent. She had stolen everything from him, his Nigger daughter and his Nigger wife. He believed in his heart she'd caused his little Lily to fall to the fever. "My family has already turned to dust. Now I'm gonna have my due." He cocked his revolver. "You stole Lela from me. And Sammie too."

"Naw that ain't it, Massa. You'se droves them away."

New Orleans, Louisiana. August 28, 1963

"MY GOD." LELA sat in disbelief, unable to comprehend it all.

Julian stared at her, waiting for her to continue. His chest tightened, fearing the worse. "Grandmère, what did Augustus do?"

Lela patted his cheek. "He gunned her down in the street, Julian. On Marais Street. Her granddaughter witnessed her murder, along with the inhabitants of New Orleans' Ninth Ward."

Julian looked down at the lawn. Why would he kill her?

But then he knew why. Augustus always kept his promises to his enemies. He shuddered, realizing he was the same way. But his own sister? Perhaps Augustus didn't know they were brother and sister.

Understanding descended upon Julian, seeing Augustus didn't care. He could only see the woman who had betrayed him. He had succeeded in eliminating all his adversaries. Julian leaned back in the swing, devastated and exhausted. Augustus had eliminated his enemies.

He shook off the dread. "Grandmère..." He didn't know what he wished to say to her.

Lela patted his knee. He held his peace.

New Orleans, Louisiana. November, 1875

SARAH FELL IN the road. After some time, once her winds returned, she opened her eyes with much labor. They were so heavy at first, but became lighter, their weight dissipating into the burden of feathers. The dust rose up around her, from where she'd landed, marrying with the humidity of the day, and then descending upon her, burying her. The screams and shouts of the onlookers floated further and further away, becoming like whispers in the garden. The animals would whisper to one another in Eden. Now she heard their whispers again.

She heard her heart, Claret, sobbing somewhere in time.

Sarah closed her eyes and then opened them once more. Dampness oozed across her chest. She relaxed.

She closed her eyes. She opened them once more. A smartly dressed White man kneeled over her. She smiled, remembering him, remembering him throughout the centuries, remembering him as they created their joy, the Rose's guardian.

Barachiel.

AUGUSTUS STOOD OVER her now dead body, titillated. He'd eliminated the Nigger bitch who had tormented him his entire life.

"Satisfied?"

He turned to his left. "What are you doing here Papa?" Augustus was losing his mind. There was no one there but the crowd of Niggers, ready to riot.

He looked down at Sarah, gloating. Soon, his gloating turned to terror, for the bodice of her dress began to inflate. He heard a sound, but he couldn't identify it. The noise grew more intense. Augustus covered his ears, unable to tear his eyes away from Sarah's growing bodice. The fabric erupted.

Augustus screamed as thousands of angry bees sprung forth from his dead sister, swarming, stabbing, and injecting him with their venom. Augustus battled them, but he was no match for the insects. Boils sprung up all over his body;

they pierced him. He ran down the streets of New Orleans, accused, convicted, and tormented by the insects.

New Orleanians gathered around where Sarah lay. One said, "She saved us when me and my'se kin was lost in dah swamp, back then before freedom came." Hearing a great buzz, the bystanders looked up to find the Queen Bee descending upon the corpse of Sarah. She came to rest upon her forehead, between Sarah's eyes, the Queen's head facing her nose. She melded her flesh with Sarah's. She died. Her twelve drones found a place to rest upon the twelve locks framing the corpse's face. Following the example of their Queen, they embedded themselves within and died, sacrificing themselves as an ornament to their fallen warrior.

Barachiel approached his daughter and wept. He dropped the roll up he'd been smoking and snuffed it out in the dust of the rue. "It is done." He stooped and scooped up his fallen child. The surrounding crowd parted, allowing him his way. Barachiel carried Sarah's body to the wagon and lay her upon its bed. Claret sat on the bench of the wagon, all but dead herself. "Come here, little one," Barachiel said.

His words enabled the child to move her lethargic body. She climbed over the bench into the bed of the wagon. She stood before this White man she didn't know. She stood above her grandmother's corpse, laid out and peaceful, adorned with bees. The White man removed a silver ring from her grandmother's finger. Claret had never noticed the ring before, a magnificent queen bee with a crown on her head. The White man slipped the ring on Claret's finger. The ring sized itself to fit her. "You will wear this ring until the day the Queen Bea comes your way. On that day you will say, 'Queen Bea born this Nigh, you will wear this ring before the Most High.'"

Claret found herself to be someone other than herself, with an understanding she couldn't explain. "Queen Bea is the Rose of the Most High. Shouldn't a Rose adorn her?"

Barachiel raised an acknowledging eyebrow and smiled. "Roses need the bees, as the bees need the roses, *n'est-ce pas?*"

Suddenly returned to the consciousness of a child, Claret began to sob, becoming hysterical. Barachiel touched her forehead betwixt her eyes. The child swooned, falling into his arms. He left Sarah's body and lifted Claret to the wagon's bench, leaning her against him, once seated. He removed his cigarette case, extracted one and lit it.

Claret awoke. Tears filled her eyes remembering the tragedy of her day, but she was no longer hysterical. "Let us take her to your uncle." Barachiel popped the reigns and turned the wagon around, returning to Claret's home.

Lela

I HAD BECOME skilled in peering through part of the drapes without being detected by callers, rather collectors. They had begun to call on us, for Jean Charles had neglected to pay our vendors. He had the money, more than enough, in fact. He just didn't care. In any case, they were simple to dodge. However, I couldn't avoid the one whom I spied exiting his carriage, charging up the steps. He pounded on the door.

"Goddammit Lela, open this motherfucking door," Augustus said.

I obeyed him. Opening the door, I then turned and ran down the hall to the library. "Monsieur?" Jean Charles met my eyes without responding. "Master Augustus is here."

"Send him away."

"She can't send me nowhere Jean Charles," Augustus said. He entered the library. "Gal, go and get me a bourbon." I obeyed him. After handing him the drink, I noticed him fan at something, as if being attacked by a fly. I took a closer look, finding a swarm of tiny bees. There must have been millions of them. I stole a glance of Jean Charles, oblivious to all. He must be able to see this. Augustus grimaced, stung by another bee. A boil sprung up were the bee had stung him. In fact, as I inspected him further, every inch of visible flesh hosted a boil. How had I not noticed his face when he walked in? He removed his hat and bees flew from beneath it.

A bee flew in attack pattern toward me. *Stop,* I thought. All of the bees, hearing my voice, vacated our home through the open transom.

"Goddamn bees. Did you see that, Jean Charles?" Jean Charles sat before him, unresponsive. Augustus scowled at his son. "Motherfucking basket case." He turned to me and looked into my eyes. *You can see them,* I heard him think. I didn't respond to him. "You're good for nothing," he said to me.

You have a moment's peace, do you not?

He raised his eyebrow. He knew he'd heard me say something, but my lips never moved. I wasn't quite sure how I'd done it; the phenomenon frightened me a bit. "You're getting to be like your goddamn Maman," Augustus said. I said nothing and returned to my unobtrusive corner of the library.

Augustus sat in the wing chair before his son's desk and refocused on the task at hand. He scowled at Jean Charles, for he had become to him the lowest life form on earth. "You've succeeded in killing me, Jean Charles." Augustus picked at a boil on his face, which burst upon his touch. "You were so busy mourning your whore you couldn't see my granddaughter was ill?"

I couldn't believe him. Then again, why should Augustus' lack of compassion for Jean Charles surprise me?

"Now, I truly have no name and no heirs," he said, bellowing at his devastated son. "It was bad enough you had a daughter and no sons. I learned to live with that. But then you let her die? You're truly a fuck up. Always have been. But then I blame myself for that, your Maman being whom she was."

"Master! That is enough," I said. "He just buried his only child one month ago, not even six months after his wife."

He punched me in my mouth.

"You little Nigger bitch." Augustus trembled with rage. *Another regret*, I heard him think to himself. "Jean Charles, you've left me with no children and no heirs. I have no other but you. You've killed me."

His cruelty could no longer hurt me. As I lay on the floor, shaking with fury, I watched Jean Charles sit at his desk, a shell. I realized at that very instant he'd entered the grave with his only child. Augustus stormed from the mansion. As soon as he crossed the threshold, his little tormentors swarmed him, entering the carriage with him, accompanying him home.

Chapter 6

La Rose Plantation. November, 1875

The driver, Johnny, stopped the carriage before the big house of La Rose Plantation. He hopped down from his bench and opened the door for Augustus. Johnny watched as his master fled the carriage and then flail about on the front lawn, swinging his arms at someone. Who was he fighting? He'd grown accustomed to strange behavior from his boss. "Somebody pro'bly done hexed him again." Johnny returned to the driver's seat and drove the coach around to the carriage house.

Augustus swung at his little attackers without success. "I've had to kill a hundred of you little bastards." He spotted Lawrence opening the front door for him.

In a final fit of fury, the bees swarmed and stung him without mercy, penetrating his clothing, and entering every orifice of his body.

"Enough little ones. Go and guard you mother."

Obeying Lawrence's command, the bees flew up and

away to the slave graveyard. The boils left Augustus. He was healed, but didn't seem to notice.

Augustus scowled at Lawrence, wishing to take his revolver and shoot him in the head. Augustus knew Lawrence was waiting to share his smart-ass comments. He wasn't in the mood for Lawrence's veiled, underhanded insults. His butler had admonished him throughout the years, in a submissive sort of way, so that Augustus couldn't accuse him of challenging his authority. Although he was a slave, nothing in Lawrence's demeanor or actions conveyed his status. In fact, as far as Augustus was concerned, Lawrence behaved as if he was his master.

"Bon Swar Massa."

Augustus could never understand his father's reasons for appointing a Nigger as the butler. However, over the course of almost sixty years, Augustus had never removed Lawrence from his charge. Augustus couldn't confute him, either. He wondered why Lawrence wasn't dead yet. He had to be one hundred years old. He suspected Lawrence had been the butler for the mansion when his father built it in the late 1700's. However, Lawrence appeared as if he was thirty years old.

"I'se guess the Lawd done blessed me with many years, Suh. Reckons I'se be here after you'se gone, too," Lawrence said to Augustus, wearied by the boy.

"Shut the fuck up Lawrence before I have to fix your flip ass mouth."

Lawrence decided to be kind to him this final time. "Massa 'Manuel is in your li'berry."

"Fuck! What's he doing here? I thought his ass had died years ago." Augustus staggered down the hall, entering his library to find it empty. "Fuckin' liar," he said. Augustus poured himself a bourbon.

He sat in his chair and leaned back. His son had destroyed him. Augustus had no heir, no name. The family name would die with him. He grimaced, realizing the statement not to be entirely true.

"You are correct, mon fils."

Augustus jumped and turned around to find his father sitting in the chair before his desk. "Where were you, Papa?"

"It doesn't matter." Emmanuel lit a cigarette.

"Decided to drop in after sixty years?"

"Can't a father drop in on his son?" Emmanuel exhaled, the smoke filling the room. "You dropped in on your son today. Dare I say your love for him has shoved him into an early grave?"

Augustus took a swig of bourbon. "Jean Charles needs to become a man. Soft little flower ass bitch. Fuck him. So what his whore died? Now, he has allowed my little Lily to succumb to the fever? A granddaughter was better than no heir at all. Now I have nothing."

"You'd curse your own Seed?"

"You already did Papa. Long ago."

Emmanuel winced. More truth lay in his words than Augustus could ever fathom. His soul remembered how Emmanuel and Mary had destroyed their family at the dawn of the millennium, once the Lord had left them.

He watched as Augustus poured the last shot the decanter had to offer. He sat the empty decanter on his desk. Augustus rested his head in his hands. He fell back in his chair, causing it to swivel. Augustus stared at the ceiling, attempting to focus. "I have no name."

"You have Lela, Augustus."

"She's a mistake. Little Nigger," he said, shoving down the knot of emotion which had sprung up in his throat. He fell forward on his desk. Augustus stretched out his hand to take hold of his tumbler of bourbon, but the glass kept moving about. He closed one eye. Two of the three glasses he saw disappeared. Augustus grabbed the one which remained and gulped down its contents.

Emmanuel sighed. Corralling his son's inebriated focus for a split second, Emmanuel locked eyes with Augustus and commandeered the attention of his soul. "Lela will bless your name, although you curse her. In that day, she will redirect you to the correct path. In that day, Lela will bear you a son whom you will curse; however, her son will bless you and this world. In that day, she will bring your son to you. In that day, he will make you whole again, healing you for all time."

Trying to make sense of it all within the convoluted synapses of his intoxicated brain, Augustus surrendered to hatred. He found it easier to curse his father's words than to receive them. "You don't know what the hell you're talkin' 'bout, Papa," he said. "How long are you staying?"

"Not long. I just wished to see you once more."

"Well, you have." Augustus finished his drink. Haphazardly scanning the room, his gaze fell upon his father. He hadn't aged. In fact, he appeared to be a young man. "What the fuck?"

Tears filled Emmanuel's eyes.

"Ass—"

Augustus' tumbler bounced upon the rug. Emmanuel arose from his place and walked over to where Augustus lay sprawled across his desk. Taking his little one in his arms, Emmanuel bewailed him. He and Camille had ruined the child once again. Emmanuel prayed the Most High would allow him the opportunity to correct Augustus once he returned to the Earth, redeeming Emmanuel from his sins against the child. Emmanuel kissed his son on the forehead, smoothing back his gray, curly locks. "Mon petit Gus." It would be many years before he would see him again. The Most High revealed to Emmanuel's heart he would give him another chance to raise up his child. All would be well.

"Why would you do it, son?" But he knew. Once again, Augustus had cursed and murdered the holy, crossing the river into the land of perdition. Augustus couldn't allow Sarah to be, unable to forgive either her or Sammie for helping Lela to escape him. After years of bidding his time, he'd succeeded in murdering his sister. Emmanuel remembered hearing Heaven's throne gasp in horror when Augustus shot Sarah dead in the street.

He wiped away his tears. "Was her sin against you so great, Augustus? You would have killed Lela if Sarah and Sammie hadn't sent her away." He watched Augustus as he slumbered. Emmanuel patted his son's head again and kissed him on the forehead. He sighed in defeat. It was done.

Do not forget, Emmanuel heard Jonathan whisper to his mind in the Spirit.

"Oh, yes," he said. Wiping away his tears for his son, Emmanuel opened the desk drawer and reached to its rear. "Ah, it's still here." Emmanuel had placed the rattle there once Augustus and Camille moved to La Rose from La Pivoine Plantation in Virginia. What was the year? Gus had to be eight years old, so 1809, perhaps?

Emmanuel admired the object, still impressed with its

beauty. When did he and Jonathan Chamberie have it made, maybe the third, perhaps the fourth century after the Lord's departure? The Lord's Magus had constructed it for them, as a result of Emmanuel's and Jonathan's repeated complaints over the centuries. The men could never soothe the highly irritable child, anointed as the Keyholder. Magus had grown tired of their whining and constructed the toy for the Keyholder, much to the surprise and delight of the men. God had answered their prayers, creating an instrument to soothe the child, granting his parents and his caretakers much needed rest and peace.

Emmanuel could still remember the moment the Keyholder held the toy in his hand for the first time. He believed the adults to be more in awe of the toy than the child. The Keyholder seemed to have the attitude of entitlement, satisfied that someone had appeased him. Typical.

Emmanuel smiled as he studied the rattle, made of solid gold, its handle engraved with coins and *fleur de lis*, embedded with emeralds. A crystal orb topped the rattle, with a gold coin emblazoned with the image of the true Caesar, *notre Seigneur*, suspended, floating, within its center.

"I wonder if it still works?" Emmanuel placed the rattle in Augustus' limp hand. Slowly, the coin began to spin within the orb. "Your energy is weak. Your time is done." Emmanuel removed the rattle from Augustus' hand and moaned, once again disintegrating into grief for his wayward son. The coin would spin for the Keyholder alone, now incarnated as Augustus, before as Evan, Jacoby, and others. However, the Keyholder wouldn't manifest his purpose for at least another one hundred years. His soul still had much to learn.

Emmanuel smiled, remembering his little Augustus playing with the rattle as an infant. The coin would spin so fast, he feared the toy would take flight! Augustus would watch it, hypnotized. He would then fall asleep, much to everyone's relief.

He believed Camille to be more fascinated by it than the child. "Where did you obtain such a thing, Manny?" She smiled and whispered to him in a soft voice while Augustus slept, taking care not to awake him. She kissed her son, and then Emmanuel.

Emmanuel wept, remembering the joyous time of his life. "It will be close to one hundred years before you hold it again, mon fils. I suspect it will be the final time," he said, smiling at his son. "Well, not quite that long."

Emmanuel broke down and sobbed once more. When had he ever cried so much? Perhaps it was his and Mary's guilt manifested in this poor soul, his Gus, which spurred his tears. "Bonsoir, my sweet Evan, my Augustus." Emmanuel kissed him once more. "May notre Seigneur forgive Mary and me."

Emmanuel departed the library and La Rose, descending the stairs to the circular drive. He entered his black coach, shutting the door. He tapped his rose signet ring, fashioned from gold, against the window.

The driver called to the team of horses. They began their slow trot, leaving the mansion. Emmanuel saw Lawrence wave to him. He smiled at him with a heavy heart. Many years would pass before he would return.

WITH TEARS IN his eyes, Lawrence watched as his brother departed. The lead horses reared back, their front legs dancing before them. The rest of the team followed suit. The driver popped the reigns and the team broke away into a full gallop. The carriage and its passenger faded into thin air before reaching the bend, disappearing from his dimension in time, from St. Helena Parish, Louisiana. Lawrence closed the door.

Chapter 7

Brussels, Belgium. November, 1875

The splendid majesty of Chamberie Consolidated reminded Barachiel of Heaven. Stopping short of Solomon's palaces, no expense had been spared when he and Jonathan Chamberie built the structure at the close of the 15th Century. Gold had been transported from the Lord's vaults around the world to adorn the walls of the seven-story, one-mile square structure. Golden friezes adorned every office to some degree, but the walls of the grand salon on the seventh floor, the receiving area for Jonathan's offices, had been constructed of solid gold. A white marble, hidden since the time of Solomon, had been quarried to construct the statues, monuments, ceilings, and floors of the seventh floor. Forty-foot marble angels propelled themselves from the four corners of the salon with their swords drawn and wings spread, challenging foes and protecting the little ones of God. Seeing the faces of his brothers immortalized in the marble statues caused Barachiel to miss them. He forever looked forward to their encounters.

The opening of the twenty-four-foot-tall doors recalled Barachiel from his admiration of the room to the one who exited from within. A smile broke across his face, seeing his little flower once more, for it had been some time. He watched as she sat at small desk to the left of the now closed double doors. The sentry resumed their stance before them, blocking all unauthorized entry.

Samaria's desk reminded him of his friend, Andre Boulle, and of Barachiel's time serving as the trusted advisor to the Sun King in the Court of Versailles. How he missed those days.

Monsieur Boulle had constructed Jonathan's enormous, twenty-four-foot-long Louis XV ormolu bureau plat desk, cast in gold and inlaid with kingwood. As a gift, Monsieur Boulle created the smaller desk for Samaria, accented with gold lilies at the corners of the desktop. Boulle used mother-of-pearl to create clusters of lilies on the front and sides of the desk. He finished the desktop with leather trimmed in gold.

Sometimes the sight of his little flower caused Barachiel heart to break, for her devotion to Jonathan had been unwavering throughout the centuries. Samaria never sought out a life outside of his. Unable to remain apart from her a moment longer, Barachiel materialized from the realm of the unseen into that of the living at entrance of the salon. Removing his pocket mirror to check his appearance, he walked over to his little flower. "Bonjour, Samaria."

Startled, she looked up from her work. She hadn't noticed anyone pass beneath the arch into the grand receiving area. "Guillet! You've returned." Overflowing with joy at the sight of her patron, Samaria jumped up from her desk and ran into his arms. Her tears escaped her, wetting his suit jacket.

"It has been many years. You're still beautiful, as always," Guillet said, comforting her.

She blushed. "God is good," she said, smiling. She removed a handkerchief from a hidden location, dabbed her eyes and then returned the cloth to its concealed pocket. "Would you care for a cognac," she asked. "It is only mid-morning, but I know it is never too early for you and Monsieur Cognac to embrace." Samaria laughed at first, but as she gazed into Guillet's eyes, finding sorrow shading them. Her smile faded. "Allow me to announce you to Jonathan, Monsieur," she said. The sentry opened the double doors, allowing her to slip in. The men closed the door and resumed their stance.

JONATHAN CHAMBERIE DRIED his eyes, overcome with Augustus' continuous goal of self-destruction, which his soul relentlessly pursued. The boy could never be happy, Jonathan realized, spurring forth a new welling of tears. "I don't know why I always weep for Evan. Well, Augustus."

Emmanuel sat before his desk, fighting back tears for his son. "It isn't his fault. But then again, it is. He must choose to embrace either love or hate," Emmanuel said. He removed the rattle from the pocket of his waistcoat. "Will you keep this for him, Jonathan?"

Jonathan received the toy from him, fiddling with it. The past flooded his memories. "I always do. I'll have Samaria place it with Hildegard's things." Jonathan toyed with the rattle for a bit, remembering the joy it had brought the Keyholder as a child, throughout the centuries. Although always an incorrigible child, the Keyholder was lovable at the same time. Yet without fail, the child always managed to mature into a hateful, possessive, and vindictive adult. His jealousy and possessiveness destroyed all those around him, especially the lives of those he loved most.

Rage mounted within Jonathan, thinking of his Lily. "I should be happy about his murder. Lily, I mean Hildegard? How could he kill her? I saw it happen in the Spirit. I felt her life slip away," Jonathan said. "After one month, Samaria forced me to get out of bed. Now I must wait. Only God knows when she will return to me." He pounded his fist on his desk. "It could be centuries before she returns."

Emmanuel said nothing.

Jonathan dried his tears. "I'm glad I'd visited her while she attended school in France. She didn't know me. I explained to her I was her family," he said, beaming with the joy of that time. "So young and beautiful, she embraced me as her cousin, showing me around *la petite ville de Fargniers*. Lela was leery of me. She didn't remember me and I could see it. Neither of them remembered," he said, recalling how they clung to one another. "They were all either of them had in the world," he said, his tears flowing once more.

"I should have taken her then. I could've taken both her and Lela. But it wasn't to be." Jonathan leaned back, surrendering into the comfort of his tufted leather high backed chair. "We must live according to notre Seigneur's will. Who are we, as men, to alter His plan? God must show Lucifer—" Jonathan stopped himself. He changed the subject, not wishing to enrage himself over matters which could neither be addressed nor changed in the present. "So, how long will you continue to carry notre Seigneur's name?"

Emmanuel raised an eyebrow, quelling his agitation. "Why does everyone have a problem with it? He has allowed it. I asked first," Emmanuel said. "What does it matter anyway? Hell, Samaria still calls me Guillet." Both men laughed as Emmanuel lit a cigarette, still obsessing over the subject. "There are men who carry the name."

"But you are not a man, Barachiel."
New Orleans, Louisiana. August 28, 1963

JULIAN TURNED TO his grandmother, confused. Sitting up, he stopped the swing. "Grandmère, what do you mean?"

Snatched from her trance, Lela crashed into the present. Her head ached. Taking a sip of water, she breathed in and attempted to steady herself, as would one who had been jarred from a deep sleep. "What?"

"What do you mean by 'Barachiel isn't a man'? Who are Barachiel and Guillet?"

Lela frowned. Perhaps she had revealed too much to him. "In Eastern orthodox scripture, Barachiel is an Archangel, Julian. He guards the Rose."

He rolled her words around in his mind. "You're saying that your great-grandfather was an archangel?"

"Julian, just listen. I do not care to be interrupted," she said.

"I asked you a question, Grandmère."

Lela scowled at the boy. "You asked to hear the story. Allow me to tell it. Listen and make your judgments once I've finished. However, if you insist on interrupting me, I will not be able to educate you effectively. So decide now what you desire. Your choice."

Julian could see he shouldn't challenge her further. She

scared him in some ways, as if she could snatch his very soul from his being and smear it into the earth, destroying him for all time. He watched as a grin crept across her face. She had read his thoughts. *Freakish mind reader.* He didn't appreciate her intimidation.

But, it wasn't truly even the intimidation that worried him. His grandmother was like water eroding a boulder away over the course of centuries. Without overt resistance, she wore down the rebellious and compelled them to accept her word without ever challenging them. Her word would be, whether others liked it or not. Julian wanted to know who Jonathan Chamberie was, but he found himself afraid to ask. Maybe he was his relative.

"I'm glad you're beginning to understand, mon cher. May I continue?"

"Yes, Grandmère."

Lela took pity on her grandson. "And to answer your question, yes, Jonathan Chamberie is related to you. Oh, and Guillet, Barachiel, and Emmanuel are one in the same. Some knew him as Guillet. Others knew him as Emmanuel."

Julian nodded in understanding. He lay his head upon her breast once more and then resumed rocking the swing. Lela leaned back, allowing the gentle glide to relax her as the motion returned her to another realm.

Brussels, Belgium. November, 1875

EMMANUEL EXHALED, FILLING Jonathan's office with billows of smoke, rising up into the rotunda mural, depicting angels tossing gold coins down to the earth, with God's creation standing beneath with outstretched hands. "Yes, it's true. I am a man but I'm not. I wasn't created in His image, as were you. While Satan and his compatriots fell due to their rebellion against God's will, I fell to protect the creation," he said. "I, along with others, such as Albertus and Zhan, fell to protect the holy families of God from the battalions of Lucifer, from whence will come Le Baton." Emmanuel took a drag from his cigarette and chased it with a sip of cognac. Jonathan always had the best cognac. He sighed, considering how his life would have been simpler as a man, living without the ability to see and know what is, protected by the Most High.

"In any case, I won't use the name for much longer. My little ones have all either left me or no longer need me," Emmanuel said. "There is no reason for me to continue to carry the name. To whom am I providing hope?" Joy descended upon him. "Yet, they've returned, but they don't know me. Can you see them, too?"

"Yes," Jonathan said, smiling.

Emmanuel became excited, watching as the Rose labored

along her path, his queen returned from the Most High. Soon, her prince would unite with her. He couldn't focus on the joy of the pending union though, with the question of his chosen name looming in his mind. Why should he change his name? "You haven't changed your name," Emmanuel said.

"I have. I haven't used my given name of Joseph since Jacoby was a child."

"Jacoby, well Augustus, was a good boy in that time," Emmanuel said.

"Yes, he most certainly was. Perhaps it was due to his limited contact with you."

Emmanuel resisted the urge to punch him. "I'm not fighting with you today, Jonathan. Anyhow, he was good for a time," he said, realizing that once he entered the boy's life, the Keyholder changed. Jonathan was right.

"I know I'm correct," Jonathan said. "In any case, there's no need for me to change my name again."

Emmanuel nodded as he fell into the Spirit, watching as the stone rolled away from the entrance of the tomb. His Lord risen, he exited the tomb. Barachiel remembered singing, praising Jesus' holy name. Mary Magdalene had spotted them both sitting atop the empty tomb, but she didn't know him. Hysteria had overwhelmed her, consumed with locating the Rabbi's missing body. His Brother addressed her, stating the infamous words, "Why do you look for the living amongst the dead?"

Jonathan smiled, observing Emmanuel's thought. "I loved notre Seigneur so. I wished for him to have peace and rest. He had suffered for sins which he hadn't committed, for he loved his creation so much. Notre Frère. I would never have dreamed the Most High would bless me so for such a small thing. God is good."

"Yes he is, Joseph of Arimathea. Your kindness to a man painted as a heretic proved to be no small thing," Emmanuel said. "Satan amazes me with his ability to sway the hearts of men." Emmanuel sat in silence for a time, considering how notre Seigneur's followers, as well as all of Jerusalem, had turned against the Savior in the final hours.

Yet, Satan's ploy proved no challenge to the Most High. Jesus conquered in spite of them all, having raised unexpected champions to comfort, encourage, and assist the Lord along his impossible path. In the end, he died and then arose from his grave to win his crown, ruling Heaven and Earth for all time.

Emmanuel released his revelry, returning to the present. "Now you keep the Most High's vaults, Jonathan. But I suppose your tenure will end once the Keyholder returns to this Earth from the bosom of the Most High." Both men sat in reflection, peering into the future, seeing their son in his glory, a financial genius, an asshole. Both men frowned, seeing all they would have to endure to raise him.

Emmanuel sighed. They would deal with the Keyholder at the appointed time. "I am now Jerémèy," he said.

"Jerémèy?"

"Oui."

"Why that name?"

"I like it. Why not?"

Jonathan considered it. The name suited him. He could see Emmanuel would carry the name until the end.

"Monsieur Chamberie?"

Roused from the vision of the future, Jonathan acknowledged her. "Oui, Samaria?"

"King Phillip has come to call."

"His appointment is today?"

"Oui. I reminded you of his visit this morning," she said.

Jonathan thought for a minute and nodded in agreement to her testimony. "So you did. Guillet's visit has distracted me. Allow me a few moments and I will receive him." She nodded, leaving them as the sentry closed the doors behind her.

Emmanuel, now Jerémèy, laughed. "Do you suppose Samaria will call me by my new name? She would never address me as Emmanuel, although I've carried the name for over one hundred years."

Jonathan laughed. "Perhaps. She refused to call you Emmanuel. She told me Emmanuel is the Lord's name and you aren't notre Seigneur." The men laughed. Samaria had been one of the Lord's most faithful servants. She stood with him until the end, witnessing his crucifixion and wailing before him as he hung on the tree.

"I suspect she's correct," Jerémèy said. "I'll leave you. You shouldn't keep his Highness waiting. He has traveled for some time to visit you here."

Jonathan laughed. "I won't extend his nation another loan. They've depleted their gold reserves. I have it all. They have nothing left to offer."

"Just once more. Once they default, take the kingdom. They're doomed," he said, looking out into the Spirit. Jerémèy vanished.

Jonathan stood up from his desk, adjusting his waistcoat.

Samaria escorted King Phillip into the opulent office. The brilliance of the room and its riches astounded the ruler. He appraised the Reuben's mural which adorned the large wall behind Jonathan's desk, depicting a lover admiring his robust beloved as the angels rejoiced about, unseen by either of them. Cupid leaned against a rock after laying down his bow, his work done.

Chapter 8

Lela

I reconsidered if I should share with him the news I'd just received from La Rose. "Perhaps it will help," I said to myself as I opened the door. "Monsieur?"

"Yes?"

"Monsieur, how are you this morning?

He stared at me, saying nothing, waiting for me to get to the point. When drunk, Jean Charles could make me feel like an idiot at times.

"Monsieur, I've received some news from St. Helena."

"What is it, Lela?"

I couldn't make myself say the words. Although he had abused me, I still remember his kindness to me as a child. I couldn't determine if I was upset. I believed I had become indifferent to him. "Master hung himself from the second floor balcony the night before last."

He peered through me as if I wasn't there.

"Monsieur, your father is dead."

He didn't respond. After a few moments I left the room, closing the door behind me.

JEAN CHARLES' DRINKING worsened. Day after day, he sat in his library, drinking into the wee hours of the morning. Over the course of the next several months, he continued his steady decline, allowing the household accounts by which he purchased food, wood, flowers, and other services to default.

His creditors began their relentless pursuit, calling upon our sad home, seeking payment. I was the only person left to address them, telling them Monsieur Chevalier wasn't well and as soon as his health improved, he would pay his debts.

All of the servants, except for myself, had abandoned him. I can't say I blamed them. If he wasn't my brother, I may have left him too. He hadn't paid any of us, not that he'd ever paid me anyway. Subconsciously, I believe he still viewed us as his property. But not really. He just didn't care anymore. I believe he wished for all of us to leave him alone to die.

At last, one year after Lily's death, I accepted the truth he wouldn't recover. Attempting to take control of our lives, to save our lives, I searched his desk for the check book. Locating it, I drafted several checks to pay all of the creditors. Early the next morning, prior to Jean Charles commencing his daily drunk, I presented the checks to him for signature.

"What the fuck is this?"

I held my temper and my tongue. He had mutated into our father. "Monsieur, we don't have any wood for the stoves and fireplaces. This is a check to pay the firewood man. He said once we have settled the account, he would deliver more. However, we must now pay in advance, since we have been in arrears for so long."

"That bastard!" Jean Charles poured himself a drink. "My family has done business with him for years. I'll find a new vendor, one who respects the Chevalier name."

I knew he wouldn't stay sober long enough to do so. "Well, in the meantime, we should settle our debt with him."

He snatched the check from me and signed it, muttering under his breath. He turned red with fury. "What the hell are these for?" He fanned about the additional checks. "Are you trying to steal from me?"

I wished to choke him, but I maintained my calm. "Those are for the general store, the butcher, the fish man, and our other vendors and merchants, Monsieur. You haven't paid anyone since, well before—"

"Shut your fucking mouth, Lela. Don't speak her name." Soon after Lily died, Jean Charles had forbidden everyone in the house from speaking the child's name. I believe he wished to forget her, although I suspected he could do little else but think of Lily.

Jean Charles gulped his drink and signed the checks. "I should have never permitted her to attend the party," he uttered weeping, his sanity escaping him before my eyes. "Why would I do such a thing? Perhaps she would have survived if I'd been stronger. I spoiled her to the point of her destruction."

I remained silent, having learned from his previous laments regarding Lily he wasn't speaking to me, but to his guilt. I stood before him, watching him weep like a little boy. I'm not sure if, at that time, I still held compassion in my heart for his loss. I had shut down emotionally by that time. I would rage within he should snap out of it. I recall shuddering as a cold chill swept through me. I'd passed judgment on him without understanding. At that moment, I believed I'd sinned in some way I didn't fully understand.

Once his tears subsided, anger contorted his face. "Leave me, Lela," he said. Jean Charles walked over to the buffet, full of empty crystal decanters. He poured whatever remained in each decanter into his hi-ball glass. He returned to his desk and turned his chair toward the a partially boarded up stained glass window, away from my piercing glare, surrendering to his own private hell.

Chapter 9

New Orleans, Louisiana. August 1963

Julian had heard enough about his grandmother's brother. He could understand him being upset, but this was a bit much. Augustus had been right, he was a weak man. Julian walked across the patio to the bar cart, finding the pitcher sweating in the sun. He poured some water into a tumbler and brought it to his lips. It scalded him. He dropped the tumbler. "What the hell?"

Lela arose from her place in the shade and joined him at the bar cart. Pouring a glass of water for herself from the same pitcher, Julian gawked at her, finding ice cubes bobbing in the liquid. He watched Lela ingest the cool drink. She smiled, refreshed. Lela returned to her place in the shade.

Julian closed his eyes and sighed. He could feel the lecture coming on strong. Without being told, he returned to his place beside his great-grandmother.

"You would judge Jean Charles, Julian?"

"What are you talking about Grandmère?" Julian said.

Lela rocked the swing. "One might say the same of you, darling." Lela turned her eyes to the upper branches of the live oak tree. In a section facing South, some of the leaves had fallen away. She wondered if the tree was in distress, for it was only August. Something deep within its being had been killing it over time. Only now had the tree begun to bear the signs of its inner turmoil. Searching within, she found a colony of pests, devouring it. *Depart this tree, for it belongs to me.*

Wondering what his grandmother was looking at, Julian turned his focus in the direction of her gaze. Tree bark? Unable to break his stare, he soon noticed the bark buckle, as if something inside pounded its way out. Within moments, a slew of beetles burst forth, falling to the ground and dying before them. Julian sucked in his breath. His grandmother patted his hand. He exhaled.

"We all have pests eating us away from the inside, Julian. Jean Charles could have released it, if he had just talked about it. He could have talked to me." Lela took a sip of water and placed the glass on the table. "Yet, he wouldn't talk to anyone. In many ways he was like his father; he didn't wish to appear weak. Instead, he used alcohol to suppress it. Yet it didn't. Drink only inflamed the issue.

"Jean Charles' father, our father, was the same way. However, father was drunk and violent." Lela furrowed her brow as she considered them both. "Jean Charles could be violent as well. However, it was different in a way, but the same." Lela turned to her child. "You are the same; however, you're not a drinker. While you don't need alcohol, you can be nasty. You would rather hurt others to protect and conceal your pain."

Julian felt the heat rise in his cheeks, flushing red. "That's not true."

Lela snorted. "There's nothing within you're suppressing, locking down and hiding away? You've dealt with all of your hurts and pains?"

"Yes."

Lela arose from the swing. "You're a liar, Julian." She watched every conceivable emotion of the human spirit flow through him. She pitied him. Yet, there was hope for her great-grandson, for her father, for her eternal adversary and love. He would get it right this lifetime. "You are my little liar, but Grandmère loves you." Julian's eyes mirrored the pain and rebellion trapped within him. She kissed him, blessing him, running her fingers through his hair.

"Grandmère must powder her nose. I will return in a few moments."

Julian watched his Grandmère assume her promenade, forever the Queen.

Epilogue

It was beautiful in the Garden on the glorious morning. La Rose allowed her blossom to open and the sun to kiss her skin. She always presented herself in the Garden as the Most High had created her, allowing her natural form to be savored by His creation.

She decided not to spend her day dreaming of her loves. "Sisters, my robe." The ladies appeared at her side, dressing her in the white, sheer garment. Although she had considered wearing nothing at all, she decided to shield herself from the dust that may waif up from her activities. La Rose placed her hat upon her head, composed of vines with red roses in full bloom. La Rose grabbed her basket and treaded down the petals of her enormous rose bush to the Earth, to her garden.

Reaching the bottom, she placed her basket containing pruners, a small watering can and fertilizer on the ground at her feet. She considered her bush and the branch which had been cut away. A pang pierced her heart; she couldn't consider the little one who had been stolen away.

But then she took heart, finding a small plant grafted into her large bush. "My lost one," she said, just above a whisper. Hearing her voice, the small graft bonded with the vine, becoming strong and vibrant. The plant grew, jutting forth from the side of her bush. Her little one lived, giving life to generations to come.

The grafted bush, now a member of the mother plant, budded. The young member put forth new branches, which immediately budded and bloomed, displaying their glory to the world. Yet, there was one renegade branch which troubled her. Before her eyes, the branch shot out and up, growing tall and strong, challenging her bush in height and authority. However, it stopped and put forth a gigantic blossom of an odd color, a reddish blue.

The Rose grabbed her basket and walked up the sturdy leaves of her own bush, until she reached the rogue blossom. The Rose retrieved her pruners from her basket. Thorns sprouted from the vines of her hat. The leaves grew larger, shielding her from the sun. She knew this blossom. He'd tormented her in her youth, throughout her existence.

"If you cut him away, I'm afraid you would lose, My Queen."

The Rose ignored the one who had materialized on the adjacent leaf, uninvited. "What do you want, Barachiel?"

He crossed over to her leaf and stood beside her, considering the reddish blue bud, yet to fully bloom. "I fear your husband would destroy me if I requested what I wished for."

The Rose positioned her pruners at the base of the stem, ready to cut the rogue blossom away. She stopped, reconsidering her decision. Much to her surprise, she found tender buds, full of love and splendor, sprouting on the stem of the reddish blue blossom.

"If you cut him away, you will destroy your vine." Barachiel walked around the blossom, stepping upon the robust leaves which surrounded it, admiring him. "Yet, he is glorious! Have you ever beheld such sharp thorns to protect a deep reddish blue blossom, encompassed with very soft petals so easily bruised?"

The Rose wished to cry. The blossom vexed her, yet encouraged and empowered her at the same time. This blossom wouldn't wilt in the heat of the day.

"No, it will not," Barachiel said. "Yet, he will prove to be poisonous to all around him. Nevertheless, he will save all in the end, n'est-ce pas?"

La Rose found his words to be true.

"Care for him. He will bloom, bringing his judgment and his seed upon this Earth," Barachiel said.

The Rose found herself alone. Without any other work to complete for the day, she continued her ascent to the top of her bush, to her flower. She retired to the comfort of her blossom, closing her petals about herself to take her rest.

Acknowledgments

I never intended to become a writer. It all happened by accident. In 1996, I had an ideal about a whorehouse in New Orleans. I wrote about two pages of text, and then stuck it in my closet. Years later, I started a new job and had fallen into a deep depression. I thought about the story – God reminded about the story. I pulled it out and started writing. I did not stop for eight years. I started in the middle, then I wrote the beginning, and marched on to the end.

I thank God Most High, who blessed me with this story, revealing to me a purpose and a talent I would have never conceived for myself.

I would like to thank Dionne Lee, Linda Banass, Ericka Dockery, Kristine Thom, Ramona L., Rebbeca Janich and especially, Victoria Smith, the first readers of my drafts of *La Rose*. Sallie Schiller referred to my books as 'The Bible."

A special thank you to my sister Dmona Ross, for reading early excerpts as I wrote the books. Thank you to Yvonne Starks. I would also like to thank Catherine Lynch, Lynn

McKinney, and William "Bill" Denton and David Murdock for reading the early edition of *La Rose,* published as an e-book. I thank Mukendi Kampuku for his advisory role on a later book of this series.

Biography.com provided me with an overview of Mrs. Tubman's life. I learned of Andre Charles Boulle from getty.edu. History.com refreshed my knowledge surrounding the details concerning the *March on Washington for Jobs and Freedom.* Background regarding Jefferson Davis and the rise of the Confederate States of America can be found at http://www.history.com/topics/american-civil-war/jefferson-davis. An account of the early life of Araminta Harriet Ross, also known as Harriet Tubman, can be found at http://www.biography.com/people/harriet-tubman-9511430#synopsis. To learn more about Toussaint Bailey's namesake, Toussaint L'Overture, please visit http://www.blackpast.org/gah/loverture-toussaint-1742-1803. The history of Marion Clemons' alma mater, the Medical Institution of Yale College, can be found at https://medicine.yale.edu/about/history.aspx

Thanks to God Most High for his Holy Word, his Son. Thanks to biblegateway.com for providing online scripture for to the world. A few references: Lot and his daughters, Genesis 19: 30-38; Rider of the White Horse, Revelation 19: 11-16; "Why do you look for the living among the dead? Luke 24: 5-6; Joseph of Arimathea Luke 23: 50-54.

I especially would like to thank those who have preserved the letter and history of Willie Lynch, a slaveholder in the eighteenth century, who instructed American and Caribbean plantation owners on how to utilize his diabolical insight into the nature of not only people of color, but of human beings as whole, to control and subdue them, thus squelching the spirit of their slave communities. By instilling a self-manifesting curse of distrust and envy into the psyche of American and Caribbean people of color, slave owners were able to gain control over their slaves, which persists amongst their descendants until this very day, over 500 years later.

Without these advocates, the truth may have been lost for all time. I believe, as Lela Chevalier Roberts stated, *"God must fix it. And we must ask Him to do so. But we can't ask Him until we can see the curse for ourselves."* To learn more about the *Willie Lynch Letter,* please visit https://archive.org/stream/WillieLynchLetter1712/the_willie_lynch_letter_the_making_of_a_slave_1712_djvu.txt, or you can initiate an internet search for 'Willie Lynch', which will divulge a wealth of information for your personal edification and review.

Works by Claudia Helena Ross

Dorothy Jones A Jazz Age Trip Through Oz
La Rose Le Baton Chronicles
La Rose Le Baton Chronicles Book II

Coming November, 2016
La Rose Le Baton Chronicles Book III

Coming 2017
La Jardin Le Baton Chronicles Book IV